HUNTER

USA TODAY BESTSELLING AUTHOR

MANDY HARBIN

For more information, please join Mandy Harbin's Newsletter!

To Kelli Reep with Flywrite Communications. Thank you so much for all your hard work getting the word out about The Bang Shift Series and for all the time and effort you put in the Diamond State Romance Authors. Now that you're an official part of the group, we're never letting you go. And it has nothing to do with your dues buying our donuts. Not completely.

CHAPTER ONE

"Can't believe you dragged me out here," Maya Carmichael muttered as she tugged on her too-short dress.

Heather slapped her hand away from the lacy hem, almost spilling her precariously handled drink in the process. "Stop. You look hot."

"Watch it," Maya said at the same time, dodging away from the amber liquid spilling from Heather's glass.

"Oops." Heather giggled as she righted her beverage. She sipped her new cocktail and waved her other hand toward the crowd. "This is what college students do. They party. Get with the program, girl."

Maya glanced around the room, feeling too exposed in the crowd. No one was paying them any attention, but still, she felt eyes on her. She always did.

For the last six months anyway.

"Chill out. If you don't quit glaring at everybody, no guy is going to come near us," Heather said, narrowing her gaze. She almost sounded sober.

Maya knew better. They'd been here three hours already and she'd lost count of how many drinks her roommate and best friend had devoured. Besides, men flocked to her, regardless of any expression Maya was sporting. Hell, her friend could be covered in garbage and dudes would just flick the maggots away to get closer.

Okay, that was a gross image.

"Easy for you to say. You don't have a crazy ex stalking you." And that was the crux of the matter. Maya wondered if she'd ever feel at ease again. She'd been so naive coming out here, thinking her parents cruel for being so overprotective. Now she missed the days of being excited about new experiences. Before she *experienced* Jake.

"Jake isn't stalking you." Heather rolled her eyes. "And I told you he was creepy. Didn't I tell you he was freakin' weird?"

"Yes," she said dryly. "You told me." Not that it had done any good. Maya had lived a sheltered life, and Jake was the quintessential bad boy she'd always wanted. He was tall, built, and inked. He rode a motorcycle, which ticked one of her extra-special bad-boy boxes, and lived by his own rules. She'd been drawn to him the second she'd laid eyes on his tight backside in leathers. But he'd been nothing like the bad boy of her fantasies. He'd been pushy at best and an outright jerk at worst. She'd been stupid enough to think the attitude came with the overall package, even felt protected when he was being possessive, cherished when he was demanding. Now, she understood him for what he was: a Grade-A asshole. He'd shown her that real bad boys were nothing like the fantasy.

They were to be avoided.

Now, if she could only find a way to get away from that particular one, she could move on with her life, forget about bad boys, even boys in general, and focus on school. Yeah, that was exactly what she needed to do.

Unfortunately, she couldn't get her roommate on the same page.

Maya took a sip of the same drink she'd been nursing since they arrived, wondering how to make the chick standing next to her understand just what she was going through.

"Sorry," Heather said. "Bad topic. Let's change it to something good. Like men who aren't total douche bags." She wagged her eyebrows, and Maya couldn't help but laugh. Heather knew how to be a goofball when there was a need for a little comic relief, but it still wouldn't sway Maya's decision and new focus in life. School. Studies.

"No men. I'm done with them," she said with a swipe of her hand, emphasizing the finality of her decision.

A horrified look crossed Heather's face. Maya barked out a laugh at the expression, which she quickly stifled since she needed her friend to take her seriously. "I mean it," she said, fighting a smile since Heather still stared at her like she'd grown four eyeballs in the middle of her face.

"You're barely twenty-one."

"I'm twenty-two."

"And you are *too* young to swear off men," she said, without acknowledging the age correction.

"Okay, not forever," she admitted. Maya had no problem being a little more realistic. "But, for now, there's nothing wrong with...you know...redirecting my focus." She shrugged.

Heather curled her lip before downing the rest of her drink. "You need to get laid."

"It's like you're not even listening to me," she said, exasperated.

"Oh, I'm listening. I'm just choosing to fix this instead."

"I don't need fixing."

"I didn't say *you*. I said *this*. Big diff."

There wasn't any difference, but Maya was too exhausted to point that out. She'd already been there past any point that girl code required she be there for her friend. "I'm gonna go."

She would try having this conversation again when it wasn't a Friday night and her friend wasn't busy getting trashed. It was a talk better suited to Starbucks, not Starlight.

"No," Heather said, her face falling. "Stay. Just for one more hour."

"Why? I'm not having fun."

"Because you're not letting yourself."

Maya sighed as she stared at the liquid sitting in her only drink of the night.

"Heather—"

"Two hours. That's all I ask. We'll dance and drink—"

"You said *one* hour."

"One's not enough."

"It'll be one o'clock by then." Just thinking about that made her fight a yawn. She downed the last of her drink and dropped the empty glass to the table. She knew a tiny part of the problem was *she* was the only one not getting wasted here. But only a super tiny part.

Heather huffed, dropping her shoulders and looking around the bar before facing Maya again. "Two hours, and if you aren't having fun by then, I won't ask you to come out with me for a month."

Maya quirked her eyebrow. Maybe this was something she could work with? Heather loved the nightlife and constantly tried dragging Maya out with her. Since things had gone to crap with Jake, Heather's attempts bordered on the obsessive. Maya could use a break from coming up with excuses to bail...or not go out in the first place. At least then her roommate couldn't plead something like "girls-night" in the name of clubbing. Maya could get the distance she needed from men without having to answer a bunch of questions. "Seriously?"

"Cross my heart." Heather smiled.

"Oh, no. I mean it. No dragging me out, no begging me to come with you, no whining when you go out without me, and no talking about possible dates. One month."

Heather frowned. "You're taking the fun out of tonight."

"I am not. I'm hashing out the details. I'll stay for two more hours. Drink. Dance. Whatever. But starting tomorrow, you *will* let me focus on what I want, which could be anything that does not involve the opposite sex."

With her hand now on her hip, Heather said, "Fine, but instead of two hours, we stay for three. We've wasted too much time talking to each other and not flirting with guys."

It was all past her bedtime anyway, and she figured this was the best deal she was going to get. "Fine."

"Yay!" Heather clapped and grabbed Maya's arm. "Let's get another drink."

And she did.

They danced, drank, and even flirted with men. Maya didn't want to be there, but she complied, making sure Heather wouldn't find fault and renege on their agreement.

By a couple of hours after midnight, Maya had even danced with two different guys—at Heather's insistence, but it still counted. One had been a little too grabby for Maya's liking, but the other one was sweet. Maybe if she weren't temporarily damaged, she could've given out her number to the psych major with blond hair...or at least been a little flirtier. But she knew she wasn't ready for that. What she was ready for was to go back to their dorm and call it a night.

"My feet are killing me." But she had to admit, once she let loose, she did have fun.

"You need to build some calluses on them."

Maya rolled her eyes and dug out her wallet to pay her tab.

"Fine. I know that look. Let me say goodbye to Brad and slip him my digits." She winked.

Maya chuckled as Heather bounded toward the guy she'd been dancing with. She tried not to laugh at his flirty pout as he got the news of Heather's impending departure.

"There you are," a familiar voice said from beside her. At least this one was charming.

"Psych major," she said, turning toward the last man she'd danced with, and smiled.

"It's Mike."

"Psych Mike does have a nice ring to it." She giggled.

He playfully groaned. "No. Just, no." She laughed harder. It was the alcohol helping her loosen up, but it wouldn't change things. Tomorrow, when she was sober and aware of Jake again, she'd revert into her shell.

Jake. She shivered. Just the thought of him had her skin crawling. She glanced around the room, feeling the hairs on her arm rise. A common reaction whenever she thought about him.

"What's wrong?" Mike asked.

"Oh, nothing." She swallowed as she looked at him again. "Heather and I were just leaving." She quickly rummaged in her wallet, but he stilled her, slipping his hand over hers.

"I took care of it already."

"Huh?" She looked up.

"Your tab. Brad and I took care of it."

"Oh, um, thanks." Yeah, she knew that was a rookie response, but she felt rusty on the whole bar-night-thing. Damn Jake and his obsessiveness. She didn't even know how to act normal around men anymore.

"You ready?" Heather asked as she walked up beside her, locking their arms together.

Maya nodded.

"Hope to see you here again next week," Mike said as Maya was being turned from him. She was glad Heather didn't give her a chance to reply.

"He's cute," Heather whispered, as much as one could in a room filled with loud music, as they made their way to the door.

"Yeah." Didn't matter. She still felt off. Hopefully, the break she was giving herself would help reset her man-clock and she could put all that Jake business behind her once and for all.

Since the club wouldn't be closing for another hour, the parking lot was still filled with cars. It had almost been filled to capacity when the two of them got there, so they'd had to park in the back. Thankfully, it was fully lit and they'd found a spot near a streetlight. Yes, she'd had a sheltered life growing up, but she wasn't completely stupid.

"Jeez, it's gotten cold," Heather said when they were halfway to Maya's car. Hers was the newer of the two, so they'd always taken it when hitting the town. And by newer, Maya meant *not a piece of shit*. Heather's car was beat up and usually got stuck in third gear. There was a trick to it, but Maya didn't like the uncertainty. She kept telling her friend one day it'd finally crap out, but Heather insisted her brother would be able to get it running again if that ever happened.

"It's fifty degrees. Hardly freezing."

"I know. Just wasn't this cold when we—oh my god."

They both froze, and not because of the chill. They stood still, gaping at Maya's car.

Her mangled, beat-the-hell-up car.

Dents over every inch.

All the windows busted out.

Jesus, there was glass everywhere.

Even the word "Whore" was spray-painted across the crunched hood.

"My car," she breathed, stumbling closer to it. What the hell happened to her car?

"Is that...? Eww..." Heather leaned away from the hood, but Maya bent down to get a closer look.

"A *condom*. Really?" And not just any condom. A used one. "What the hell?"

Maya's car was destroyed. Totaled.

"Who would do—"

Ice ran through Maya at the first name that popped into her head.

"It could've been anybody," Heather said quickly, shaking her head and obviously reading Maya's thoughts.

"He's the only one with a grudge," Maya said, backing away instinctively.

"Even Jake isn't this big of a dipshit."

Maya blinked, feeling her eyes getting wet, and stared at her friend. "That's just it. I think he is," she said, her voice getting smaller.

She looked at her car again and wanted to bawl. What was she supposed to do now?

Heather rubbed her head and looked around the car while Maya's head swam. "What's this?" Heather asked as she leaned into the broken window.

"Don't." Maya leapt toward her and pulled her away. "Don't get too close to it. In fact, we...we should go back inside. Call the police."

"That wasn't in there before." Heather said, pointing toward the spot Maya had pulled her from.

Maya shook her head.

"I'm serious," Heather said, pulling free of Maya's desperate grip.

She looked closer without moving to see what her friend was talking about. There was a piece of paper on the seat. A sudden surge of adrenaline rushed through her.

"It looks like a note."

Yes, it did.

As if she was moving without conscious effort, Maya reached in to get it.

And read it.

"No," she breathed, crumpling it in her hands.

"What?" Heather asked, grabbing her arms and forcing her to focus.

"Jake," she breathed. "I think...I think he's much worse than I thought."

"Um, no really?" Heather asked sarcastically. "Look at your car."

Oh, god, this was bad. This was very, very bad. She had to get out of here. What if he was still around, watching, waiting? "I gotta go." She turned to leave.

"Where?" Heather asked, grabbing Maya's arm.

"I don't know, but I can't stay at the dorm. Neither can you. He knows our room number. We have to...have to stay somewhere else until he's arrested. You have any family around here?" Her thoughts were racing as she tried to come up with a plan.

Heather shook her head frantically. "You know I don't.

I'm from Arkansas. All I have left is my brother, and he's back home, six hours away."

"Mine is in North Carolina, but I can't go back home with this. You know how big of a fight I had to put up to get my parents to agree to an out-of-state school." She bit her lip and looked around. Her choices were extremely limited. "I'll just have to report this and see if we can be assigned another dorm." Yeah, that would work. Her parents wouldn't have to know.

Before she changed her mind, Maya called 9-1-1 and reported the damage to her car. It didn't take long for the operator to take down the information and ensure her a police unit had been dispatched. When she ended the call, she saw Heather tapping on her own phone beside a nearby tree.

"What are you doing?"

"Calling my brother."

"What?" Maya screeched, grabbing the phone. "It's after midnight." Heather rarely talked about her brother, Hunter, but when she did, she never failed to mention how much of a hard ass he was.

"It makes the most sense. We can't afford to stay at a hotel until this blows over. I'm not asking my brother for the money, and we can't use your parents' emergency credit card. Too many questions and too easy to get caught up in lies." Wow, Maya hadn't even thought that far ahead yet.

"We can't be out of school more than a few days. We'll get behind," she warned.

"I know. It's a long drive, yes, but one we can make again the minute that asswipe gets locked up. We'd be back in class the next day."

Maya groaned, knowing she didn't have much of a choice. It was either that or stick around here where she didn't feel safe. At. All. "Fine. Just wait until tomorrow to call him, though. We still have to talk to the cops, and there's no telling how long that'll take. Neither of us is in for a drive like that tonight anyway." Although they'd stopped drinking a while ago, they'd been dancing the night away. They'd be too exhausted making that trip right now. Besides, maybe by tomorrow, Maya could think of a better idea. She'd never met Hunter, but what she did know about him did not give her any feelings of reassurance.

She'd met her life quota of jerks already.

"Yeah, you're right." Heather dropped her phone back into her bag and leaned against the tree. "But I'm calling him tomorrow." Was Maya that transparent?

She sighed, knowing she probably wouldn't be able to come up with an alternative before they had to hit the road. She would try, though. She glanced at her car again. Ugh. No ideas were coming to her yet. "He's not going to like this." She didn't know the man, but something told her it was true.

Heather pinched the bridge of her nose. "No. He's gonna be pissed."

Great. *Just great.*

CHAPTER TWO

THE HAUNTING scent of exotically roasted kernels suffocated Hunter while he slept. An aroma pleasing to others—especially the scores of women eager to run their hands through Rudolph's hair, his Argan-oil infused, pomade-coated hair—triggered Hunter's gag reflex more often than not. No high-end styling product in the El Paso area was good enough for Rudolph. He ordered that stinky shit from his home country of Brazil. If Hunter had first smelled it on a sexy woman, the now-offending scent probably wouldn't have even registered. He wasn't one to pick up on things like that under normal circumstances.

Alonzo Rudolph was anything but normal, and Hunter would never forget the smell he associated with his former boss.

No matter how many years had passed.

He kicked a leg free as he turned in his bed. He knew he was dreaming about his time in El Paso. A time he fought to forget. He usually succeeded during the day, but nightmares were harder to beat.

"You owe me money," Alonzo said, using the tip of a

knife to clean under one of his fingernails. Hunter didn't understand how the man could be so cool while another sat helplessly tied to a chair. Hunter didn't even know the man's name who sat bruised and dirty in his own piss. It made it easier.

Less personal.

"Please," the man choked.

Alonzo gave Hunter a bored glance. "You know what I want, *criado*."

He did. As a *criado*, a servant, he knew his orders. He took out the wire cutters from his pocket and grabbed the man's pointer finger.

"Maybe next time you'll learn to pay your bets," Alonzo said before giving Hunter a slight nod, the signal to cut off the man's finger.

Hunter muttered in his sleep, shaking his head, but in his dream, he was as calm as he'd been expected to be. With a quick snip, the man screamed, and still he heard Rudolph mumble, "That's a good *criado*," giving praise he did not want.

The suffering man's blood-curdling cries grew louder, but Hunter soon realized the sound had morphed into his own roar as he jolted up, awake, in a cold sweat.

He grabbed his heaving chest.

"Jesus Christ," he panted as the dream disintegrated and reality slowly returned.

But it wasn't a dream. It was a memory. One of many he'd be forced to live with since fleeing from Rudolph.

Alonzo Rudolph, the Columbian gang enforcer who'd tried recruiting Hunter into his drug-trafficking crime family.

He'd very nearly succeeded.

The alarm sounded beside him, and he cursed as he hit

the snooze button and fell back. He needed a minute before he showered and headed to the garage.

With his poor upbringing, the never-ending cash and women had been too great of a temptation for him when he'd been in his early twenties. Hunter hadn't been a Boy Scout by any stretch of the imagination, but he'd had morals, and it was ultimately his good core that had stopped him from turning to a life of seriously-fucked-up crime—no matter how much he'd needed the money. The taste he'd been given those few short months had been too much for him. He'd wanted out before ever getting in, quickly seeing it would lead to more harm than any good the cash could bring. Cutting ties and moving back home had been easy since he'd been smart enough to hide his real name and life outside of El Paso, wanting to keep his sister safe at least until he'd found his way and could ensure her protection in that life.

Unfortunately, Rudolph wasn't one to take no for an answer. He had means, and Hunter knew there was a time when he'd come to collect. It didn't matter that as the years went by and Hunter got even more entrenched with the Bang Shift, fighting on the *sort of* right side of the law, he was stronger and smarter than he was at nineteen. There was still a small part of him that hoped Alonzo Rudolph would forget about him and not waste any energy on disciplining a boy who no longer existed.

But beneath Hunter's jokester attitude and life at the shop was a man who knew the price of breaking loyalties, and when that debt was due to a man hell-bent on collecting anything owed to him—especially from a *criado*—Hunter knew it would never expire.

He just didn't know when the man from his past would come to collect, busting his life wide open and exposing a part of him Hunter wished more than anything would stay buried forever.

He didn't have time to worry about that right now, though. He was already late for work. By the time he'd shaken off the last remnants of the dream and dragged his ass out of bed, it was already time he should've been pulling into the garage. He'd planned on tying his hair back, tugging a ball cap on, and foregoing the shower to make up time, but after one long look at the straggly mess on his head, he decided he'd had enough of it. He'd dug out his clippers and started shaving some of the crap off. His hair was still messy, but at least it was off his neck. He'd cleaned up his bathroom and showered to get the loose hairs off him. He was forty-five minutes late by the time he walked through the opened overhead door into the one of the bays.

"Dude."

He wasn't sure which one of the guys called out.

"I know I'm late," he said over his shoulder.

"No. The hair."

Hunter chuckled when he finally recognized Blade's voice. "Needed a change," he called out as he looked at the board that listed all the cars scheduled to be worked on and their issues. A couple of oil changes, a realignment, Toby needed new rotors and brakes, Mrs. Bell needed a new transmission... He stopped reading the rest, deciding he'd check on that.

"Tranny in?" he asked as he turned.

Blade wasn't the only one gaping at him. Brutus—*Brody*. He'd dropped the nickname Colonel had given him, but Hunter still had a hard time remembering not to use it— held an impact drill poised at a lug nut. Gauge stood in a well underneath one of the oil changes. Roc, the little shit, sneered at him as he twirled a wrench. Bear stood in his office, hands on his hips, staring at him through the window of walls that separated the executive staff from the grease monkeys.

Yeah, all gazes on him.

"What?" he asked them, but he kept his focus locked on Bear. He was their boss, after all. Well, he was now.

Once Colonel's double-crossing deeds had been exposed, the garage he'd bought and used as a cover for his team's activities had been seized by the government. The feds decided to orchestrate a sale of Shepard's Garage to Bear. On paper, the big bald man was the new owner and they were all his employees.

As part of the deal, the garage got a facelift, some new equipment, and after very little debate, a shiny new name. They figured the townspeople would feel awkward using a business that was in any way linked to a criminal, and branding it something different would help solidify the change of ownership.

Bang Shift.

Naming it that was a nod to the guys' little inside joke, which they all thought was pretty fucking awesome.

It'd been the right move. Business was definitely booming, with regular jobs coming in from as far as White County. They still worked on everyday cars, but they were also becoming known throughout the state as specializing in hotrods. Working on those antique muscle cars was a wet dream, but none of the men would forget the shop's real purpose—a working front for their *other* job.

Yeah, there'd been much discussion about that, too. Colonel, a.k.a. Jeff Coleman, had started it, but truth was, they'd been doing this for years, and they could still serve a vital purpose. Besides, they all liked kicking ass and taking money. Being a hired special ops team definitely had its perks, and whether he worked on American muscle or squeezed his nine on the government's dime, Hunter loved both jobs equally.

They all did.

Bear stormed out of the office. "Everybody to the meeting room."

Okay, maybe there were *some* parts of the job Hunter hated. Like meetings. Bear might be pretending to own the shop, but he was their *real* boss. Team lead appointed by the feds, and voted in by the guys for all other jobs. The man did have the most experience, even if Brody had pointed out he was now the oldest in the group. The guys knew he'd just been ragging on Bear and didn't really want the responsibility that came with the job. Hunter hated all the bureaucracy, but he understood the need for a point man, someone to oversee their options, both in the garage and out. Bear really was the perfect man for the job.

"Glad you decided to join us today," Bear muttered as Hunter walked by. "Head get stuck up your ass?"

"Yep, had to cut my way out," he said, pointing at his newly cut hair.

Bear cracked a smile but quickly suppressed it as the guys filed in and took their seats. "Now that pretty boy is here—"

"Hey, I was ten minutes early," Blade said, patting his boyish face. "And I fix my hair everyday," he added with a shrug. His spiky blond hair looked as if it could cut someone if he rammed the person just right, a far cry from his brown mop.

"No one's taking your pretty boy status, man," Brody said, clapping Blade on the back.

"Good 'cause I'd be all hurt and shit."

"He shaved his head," Gauge said, cutting his gaze to Blade. "Let the man have a moment."

"I shaved my balls. Does that mean we get to focus on me again?" Blade asked.

"Can you see your pussy better now?" Roc asked with a smirk.

"Fuck you."

"Not even on a Tuesday, my brother." Roc crossed his arms, his stare daring.

Roc, *Jesus*, Hunter wished the man would just quit and leave the country. If he wasn't so good at what he did, Hunter would be the one screaming the loudest to drop his ass. Dude thought he was better than everyone, and he had a serious problem with authority.

Hell, even people in general.

"Enough. I didn't call y'all in here to trash talk." Everyone stopped joking and focused on their boss. Roc even gave the superior his undivided attention. "Thankfully, we don't have any external contracts right now, because we have mechanical work out the ass. I have two big deliveries coming next week, both classic restores. We need to knock out what we have going on so we can focus on those."

"What's coming?" Gauge asked.

"'62 Porsche and '55 Chevy wagon."

"Nomad?" Roc asked, real interest in his eyes.

"Yep—"

"I want it," he said, cutting off Bear.

"The fuck you say. What makes you think *you* get to tinker with the Nomad?" Gauge asked. "I've wanted to work on one of those for years."

"Dude, you didn't know what a fucking wrench was a

few years ago," Brody said, calling out the man who'd come to the shop as an undercover FBI agent.

"And I fucking called it," Roc said.

"This isn't the playground. Why don't you act your age?" Hunter asked. *Damn juvenile asshat.*

"Your momma thought I acted my age real good last night," Roc muttered.

Hunter saw red. It was one thing to insult a man's mother. It was something else entirely when that mother was dead. He leapt out of his chair and lunged for Roc.

"Whoa." Gauge moved lightning fast, wrapping himself around Hunter to stop him from attacking. Brody and Blade reacted almost as quickly by jumping between the two men, creating an even bigger obstacle for Hunter.

"C'mon, asshole," Hunter taunted as he struggled to break free from Gauge's steel-like arms.

"Dude, not cool," Blade said toward Roc. "You know his parents are dead."

"Mine too. So what?" Roc said before looking at Hunter. "Any time. You name it."

A loud crash sounded, causing Hunter's attention to shift. Bear stood by his desk with a broken laptop barely hanging onto the edge. "Sit—*the fuck*—down."

Roc was first to relax his stance and take his seat, either not caring about the threat Hunter presented or trusting he'd follow orders too. Hunter wasn't sure which way he wanted to go.

"Now," Bear said, clipped.

"It's all good," Blade whispered, nudging Hunter to sit. Once he did, the others followed suit.

"Roc, you and I are having words after this," Bear announced, though Roc didn't seem fazed by it.

After a few seconds of the men staring each other down, Bear turned toward the rest of the guys.

"We'll handle those assignments when they come in. We have too much other stuff to work on in the meantime." Bear went through all the current work, who'd be doing what, and even touched on the jobs they had on the calendar for the next several weeks. When he finished discussing the shop's duties, he turned to Brody. "How's Xan doing?"

Brody smiled and Hunter felt gut punched. He'd never known what that feeling was like—to love someone so completely—except when it came to his sister, Heather, but she didn't count. As much as he loved her—and he did completely—she almost equally pissed him off. Why wouldn't she grow up already? The girl was away in college, barely getting passing grades, and partying all the damn time. Despite his frustration with her...he envied her. Envied the youth that had been stolen from him.

"Good. She's ready for summer, and I don't have the heart to remind her how hot it got last year. Scott's ready for summer too, but just because he's itchin' for school to be out. He and Chad got accepted into some elite football camp. Don't know how she'll cope with her baby boy gone. Roxie, either, for that matter." He chuckled.

"Look at you, all domestic and shit," Blade said, grinning from ear-to-ear.

Hunter didn't miss the slight widening of Bear's eyes at the mention of Roxie. He had no idea what was going on between the two of them, if anything. Hunter was the only one of the group who'd grown up around here. He'd known Roxie since they were little. She'd had a bad go of it with Chad's dad, but she seemed to be doing okay now. Sweet lady. If he hadn't remembered her in pigtails, and if Bear hadn't been sniffing around her the moment he moved here, Hunter might've considered hooking up with her once or twice after seeing her out at the bars. He knew better, though. Men didn't poach, even if Hunter wasn't sure Bear had staked any claim on the woman.

"I'm a changed man," Brody said, leaning back in his chair and putting his hands behind his head. "Even Roc can't rain on my parade."

The guys chuckled.

Roc cracked a smile. It was more of a we'll-just-see-about-that smile than one of actual joy, but it was still a grin.

It was amazing to him just how much changed in the last year. Maybe it was the betrayal of someone so close to them, but all the guys seemed a little closer to each other as a whole than back when Colonel was over them. Even the asshole Roc, just barely.

Hunter's phone vibrated, so he dug it out as Bear said something that made the guys chuckle again. When he looked at the screen, he bit back a curse, knowing he couldn't ignore the call.

"Be back in a sec," he said as he stood, accepted it, and made his way out of the room for some privacy. "Hello?"

"Bubba?"

"Yeah, Heather, what's up?" he asked as he closed the door behind him.

"Oh, thank god. I've tried calling you all morning."

Huh? He hadn't had any missed calls from her, had he? Then again, one missed call from her might as well be a dozen. Good thing she couldn't see him rolling his eyes. "Is everything okay?" he asked, knowing it wouldn't sound anything but concerned.

"No. Everything is not okay. Maya's ex-boyfriend like totally vandalized her car. She's been saying he's stalking her, but I've been telling her she's nuts—sorry, but I thought you were," she said away from the phone, which meant she wasn't alone. "Then we went out to Starlight last night, but while we were in there, he trashed her ride. I mean beat it the hell up. Wrote hateful things on it. Even left a *used* condom on it, Hunter. How sick is that?"

He pinched the bridge of his nose as he tried to make sense of her words. "Who?"

"Jake."

"No, I mean who are you with? Who's this Maya?"

"Oh my god, do you never listen to me? She's my roommate. Practically my best friend. We had to call the cops. They came out, and we told them about Jake, but they said they have to investigate it. I don't think they believed us."

"Slight right turn in two miles," a monotone voice announced in the background.

"Don't let me miss the exit," Heather said, and Hunter knew she wasn't talking to him.

"What's going on? Where are you going?"

"Home. To your house, I mean."

He stood straighter. What the...? "You're coming here? You can't miss class, Heather." Boy trouble with some misfit wasn't reason enough for her to ditch. For all he knew, she was reaching for an excuse not to go.

"He threatened her," she said softly, but he didn't miss the quiver in her voice. "He knows where we live. We've left a message with the dorm monitor—"

"Wait. He's been to your room?" he asked, a chill creeping down his spine. And only partially because of what she was telling him. His baby sister let boys into her room? At night? He didn't like the thought of that at all. And now some jerk who'd been that close to her was causing problems?

"They were dating. Of course he has."

"And now he's vandalized her car," he said evenly, not really asking. Hell, if the asshole had the nuts to take a bat to someone's car, what was stopping him from doing the same to someone's face? Like his sister's. How the hell had she gotten in the middle of something like this? "Where are you?"

"Arkansas," she said slowly. So she was over the state line, meaning she was already over halfway to Mayflower.

"Get your ass here. Now."

She sighed. "We're trying. We left a few hours ago. Should be there sometime after lunch."

"Go to the house. I'll be there."

"Hunter—"

"No, Heather. We'll talk when you and your friend get here. Go straight to the house. Nowhere else. I know how long the drive takes. I mean it. I'll start driving in your direction if you're not here by one."

"Fine." It almost sounded as if she called him a name as she hung up, but he was too focused on this new development to care about his sister's petty behavior.

Someone had taken out a car she'd been in? The perp knew where she lived? How well did she know this man? And was she blowing this way out of proportion? Sometimes he didn't know when it came to her and her dramatic personality.

He pocketed the phone and went back into the meeting room. The guys were talking about some Mustang restore, but quickly quieted and looked to him.

"My sister's on her way. She might be in trouble," he hedged.

He'd take care of her. He always would. But whoever this Maya chick wasn't his responsibility. She must've been an even bigger handful than Heather if she was bringing around this kind of trouble. But his sister was right to call him. She was aware he was capable of fixing things.

Heather knew a little about his *other* job. She wasn't completely in the dark about his present life. His past? Yes, but not his current jobs. Which meant she sure as hell understood he had to keep that side of his life private. An unknown houseguest, no matter how short the duration, was unacceptable. If they were in real trouble, he'd help the girl get home, but that would be the extent of his generosity toward her. He had too much at stake.

"What do you need from us?" Bear asked, his stern expression matching the rest of the group. Men who'd grown to be brothers to him. Well, all except Roc. He was a prick.

"Don't know. She'll be here in a few hours. I'll assess what's going on and get back to you."

"You do that," Brody said, clenching his jaw. Hunter knew he was worried just as much about Hunter's sister as he was any danger she could be bringing with her...and to Xan's doorstep. Brody was overprotective of his little bunch. Rightly so.

"No worries." But with his sister, nothing was ever easy. He just hoped this threat wasn't as serious as she was making it out to be.

Maybe one day he'd finally be able to read her.

Today was not that day.

CHAPTER THREE

"HE WAS MAD. I know he was," Maya said again. She'd been saying it for the last two hours or so, ever since Heather had gotten off the phone with her brother.

Not that her friend had paid much attention to her musings.

"We should've had the police contact the dorm rather than leaving a message with the dean," Maya tried again. "Lindsey would've understood the predicament and reassigned our rooms." Surely she would have. But no, they had to jump in an old car and drive to another bruiser's house. In another state. Just because Hunter was Heather's brother didn't mean he wasn't a big badass with an attitude problem.

In another state.

Heather smirked and turned up the radio. Gah. Why was that chick so calm when she was about to sweat through her shirt? Literally. Like she needed a shower before she got close to anyone. But she couldn't worry about hyperactive sweat glands when her thoughts were racing as fast as Heather was driving this car.

She squeezed her eyes shut in an attempt to push the negative thoughts from her mind. When she opened them, she watched the green of the trees zip by. Maybe if she wasn't so stressed out, she could enjoy the road trip. The state was covered in late spring growth, but Maya didn't have the patience to enjoy anything visual, not when she was worried about meeting Heather's brother.

And what Jake would do next.

And how her parents would react if they found out she hadn't told them about her car.

And worried about getting lost on some back road.

In. Another. State.

The radio volume dropped. Maya looked at Heather questioningly. "He's fine. I know my brother. His bark is worse than his bite."

"I don't like barking either."

Heather rolled her eyes. "I mean, he's harmless." She coughed. "If he wants to be," she said as she looked out the side window.

"What does that mean?" Maya screeched.

She shrugged and faced the road again. "I mean, yes, he's big and strong. You know that. But, er, there's something you should know about him."

"What?"

"He's in the military. Special ops kinda stuff. I-I haven't said anything before because he's not allowed to talk about it. I don't ask questions. It seems to work. I just wanted you to know so you don't pry into his business."

"Oh my god. That information would've been useful when we were deciding to go to his house."

Heather laughed. "No way. If I'd said something earlier, you wouldn't have come."

"No kidding. I've seen the Military Channel." It took a special kind of man to even join the military. But those elite groups were apparently filled with an even more specific type—the type that didn't take crap from anybody. And here she was on her way to his house?

"You watch too much T.V."

"No, I don't, and what about him being a mechanic? Did you lie about that to cover it up?" Maya asked, barely realizing she was fisting her hands together.

"No, no. He does work at a garage. But he gets called on missions when he's needed."

She felt the blood drain from her face as reality slowly clicked. He was really *dangerous*. Not some bad boy pretending to be tough. Heather's brother was a dangerous man. She turned to stare blankly out the windshield.

"At least you know he's not the type to trash your car," Heather said softly.

"No," she said tonelessly. "He's the type to hide in a bush and slit a man's throat in the still of the night."

"Good lord, you *do* watch too much T.V." Heather sighed. "He's a good person. He helps people. That's all you need to think about, okay?"

All she needed to think about? Nope, not even close.

Maya decided to keep her mouth shut for the last forty-five minutes of the drive. But her brain and her armpits never slowed. She wasn't ready when they exited the highway, nor when they turned down a narrow road. After another few minutes, Heather maneuvered the car onto a dirt path, a death knell echoing in her mind as they drew closer to the only house in sight.

"We're here," Heather unnecessarily announced as she killed the engine.

A shiny motorcycle and a dirty old truck sat under a detached carport. Typical male.

Typical *bad boy* male.

Her palms began to sweat too. Wasn't bad enough she was too scared to take off her light sweater in fear of finding sweat stains that'd put a linebacker to shame. She had to show nerves in other bodily places now. Great.

"C'mon." Heather patted her arm before easing out of the car. Maya didn't have any choice but to follow her. After grabbing their bags from the truck, they made their way up the porch, but she couldn't look. She watched her feet as they trekked the last stretch of their trip, knowing there was no turning back.

Maybe this won't be so bad, she thought frantically as Heather opened the door and went in ahead of her. It wasn't as if they were staying for a long time. Just a few days at most. He probably wouldn't even be here most of the time.

She wasn't sure if she believed the impromptu pep talk, but she'd clench the straw she'd grasped and not let go.

"Now what the hell's going on?" a deep voice boomed, and any shred of hope was completely dashed. *Crap.*

"Good to see you, too, bubba."

Maya watched as Heather dropped her bag. She gently placed hers on the floor beside Heather's purple-glittered one.

"Don't bat your eyes at me, Heather. I'm not Dad."

"Oh my god, you finally cut your hair. Quit being such a bear and hug me." Heather moved and Maya mustered the strength to look up.

The air in the room disappeared, sucked away from one look at Hunter Anderson.

Oh, she'd seen photos of him, so she knew he was good-looking, but those images didn't do him justice. He wasn't just sexy. The man was downright stunning.

And he was staring right at her.

She wanted to glance away, but she was trapped, held captive by his puppy-dog brown eyes that seemed to contradict his hard body.

"I want to know everything," he said, and oh my god, that voice...so deep. When he'd spoken, he'd not looked away from her. Was he talking to her or his sister? And why was he not moving? He just stood there while Heather squeezed him into an embrace.

Should she respond? She opened her mouth, not sure what to say, but in that moment, he seemed to unfreeze, wrapping his arms around his sister and hugging her back.

Holy wheat crackers, his arms were freaking huge. They flexed then, riveting her, and any saliva left in Maya's mouth vanished. She wasn't sure if it was because she was freaking out by the size or impressed by it. Neither was acceptable. She swallowed a few times to moisten her mouth, but wasn't having much luck. Her tongue was sandpaper. She'd probably sweated out all of her body's liquid reserves on the trip here. If she didn't get a drink soon, she probably wouldn't be able to speak, which wouldn't surprise her in the least considering everything she'd been through. Plus, she needed to get a breather away from this man's penetrating gaze. Which was horrible in and of itself since she'd only been in the same room with him for a matter of seconds. But she needed a minute to herself like right now.

"Er, I need to pee?" What? Why had she said *that*? Was she bouncing now for the full effect? What was wrong with her? She should've asked where the kitchen was so she could get a drink like she really needed. She couldn't pee right now even if she had to.

Hunter pointed to the side as he let go of Heather. "First door on the right."

Maya couldn't say anything else. She didn't even acknowledge the direction she'd been given with a nod of approval or anything. She darted down the hall and into the bathroom, shutting the door behind her. Water from the faucet blasted out and onto her sweater when she turned it on, but she didn't care. She splashed the cool liquid on her face and drank a few sips from her hand.

It smelled like eggs. She wrinkled her nose and lifted away from the sink to stare at her dripping reflection.

She was really at Heather's brother's house. Why had she gone along with this?

The guy was seriously hot. Like holy-cow-he-could-be-a-model *hot*. Why did he have to be so man-pretty? It should be a crime to look like him. She groaned, hoping the sound of the water covered her. She knew right then she was going to have to stay in there until she pulled herself together, no matter how long it took.

If she could re-do this day, she'd have pulled up her big girl panties and called her parents. Told them everything.

Pleaded with them not to yank her from school.

But she was here now. She'd fled from one bad boy...

And into the den of another.

———

HUNTER WATCHED Maya practically run to the bathroom. She had a nice ass, which pissed him off. He'd already mentally noted how beautiful she was, even after a long—and apparently sweaty—car ride. Her curly hair was wet at the temples, but she showed no other signs of physical discomfort. He could see the panic in her gaze, though, but it only made her more appealing. He didn't have to know her to see how absolutely breathtaking she was. Not that it mattered. The woman was his sister's friend and possibly in some trouble. Which meant, she might have put Heather in danger, and that was a big strike against her, no matter how hot she was.

"Start talking," he said, drawing his attention away from the direction Maya had gone.

"What made you decide to finally do it?" she asked, reaching for his shorter hair.

He jerked back. "Now, Heather."

"I told you on the phone that we—"

Hunter sliced his hand through the air. He didn't want the information pieced out to him. She'd done that already on the phone, but he wanted every detail. "From the beginning."

He pulled her toward the couch and nudged her until she sat.

"Fine," Heather sighed, and started the tale of what had happened last night. Hunter gritted his teeth and tried to focus on the facts. And not the ones relating to his sister going to a bar to pick up dudes. Yes, she was legally an adult, but he still had a hard time seeing her that way.

"So you went out, got drunk, planned on driving back to your room inebriated, walked across a dark parking lot, alone, in the middle of the night, and possibly stumbled onto a crime in the making with the bad guys still lurking around. Did I get that right?" he asked. His voice raised with each word. Shit, were his ears red? They felt like they were on fire.

Heather shrunk back a little. "Well, when you say it like that, it sounds bad."

"It *is* bad. Jesus, what were you thinking? You could have been raped, stabbed, killed."

"You're blowing it out of proportion."

"Really? Because *you're* the one who felt the need to drive for hours to get away from the guy." He shook his head and looked away. "This is why I didn't want you going to school out of state," he muttered. And especially not in Texas. Though he couldn't add that little part. At least Dallas wasn't near El Paso.

"Oh, please. You needed me tucked away someplace safe while you go rescue kidnap victims and stuff. Don't turn this around on me," Heather snapped.

"Shhh, your friend can't know about that," he whispered heatedly.

Heather smiled and cocked her head to the side. "Don't worry. I took care of it."

Hunter shut his eyes slowly, searching for patience and finding little. "How did you manage to do that?"

"I told her you were in the military. You know, special ops. That you go out on missions. Which you do, so it was the perfect explanation."

"You lied and told her I was in the military?"

"Yes."

He stared at her incredulously. "And just what did you tell her I do for them?"

She shrugged. "I didn't. I told her, because of that, not to ask about your job and stuff. It was private, and we don't even talk about it." She smiled. "See, it works because if something comes up and you have to leave before we do, there's no explaining that has to happen. And if we're all just sitting around, she won't accidentally bring up something she's not supposed to."

So now his sister was lying about him. *Lying.* No, she couldn't tell anybody about the work he did for the government and the private sector, but that didn't mean she had to make shit up. Whatever happened to letting someone know when something wasn't their business? It should've been as simple as that.

But now he had to pretend to be something he wasn't.

"Just what branch of military did you tell her?"

Heather frowned. "I didn't specify. You're in one that does special ops, though."

"Fuck, they *all* do one way or another. I've never been in the damn military. How am I supposed to know how to act around her?" He stood and towered over Heather. "Never mind. Doesn't matter," he said slowly.

"Why not?"

"'Cause she's not staying."

Heather jumped up. "Yes, she is. We drove a long way to get away from that bozo Jake. As soon as he's apprehended, we can go back. It won't take them long. It's not like he's hiding somewhere. He's too arrogant for that."

"You cannot be that naive." No one could be that clueless. "Heather, the cops have to do an investigation. Sure, they could question that boy, but if he doesn't confess, they won't have anything to hold him on. They'd have to wait for results on all the tests they conducted. That shit takes time. It's not like CSI."

"And you said I watch too much T.V.," Maya said from behind them. Hunter turned, zeroing his gaze on her as she stood in the entryway of the hall.

"How much did you hear?" Jesus, if she heard about the military lie, he'd have to figure out how to fix it and fast.

Otherwise, he'd have to let the guys know. Damn Heather and her trying to help. She should've kept her mouth shut.

"From the part where you said I can't stay."

Heather socked him in the shoulder, but the tightening in his chest hurt more. God, he hated that sad look in Maya's eyes. He hated even more that he cared at all.

"We're sticking together," Heather said. "If you go, I go."

Hunter glared at his sister. The hell she was, but he knew better than to say it like that. "You're not helping." When he looked toward Maya again, she'd walked closer to them. "It's nothing personal. I don't mind making some calls and finding out what's going on. If it's serious, I'll get you on the first plane to your parents' house."

"Bubba—"

"No, Heather," he said, cutting his gaze to her.

"Hunter, we're sticking together."

He growled low and slow as he thought quickly, but no answers came to mind fast enough. The only thing he could decide on was that he was the one in the room who needed help now. Placating his sister and her hot friend wasn't going to get them anywhere anytime soon.

"I'm going to talk to some friends. You two stay put." He grabbed his motorcycle keys, hoping the cool air would ease his anger, and fired off a text to Bear to warn him and the guys he needed to see them. Just what he needed—another meeting. He marched toward the door as he shoved his phone in his pocket.

"Nice introduction," he heard Maya mumble to Heather.

He looked over his shoulder before he could stop himself and said, "Hunter Anderson."

Her light eyes popped. And yeah, he was a dick for liking that he startled her. "Maya, um, Carmichael."

"There. Now we're practically family, Maya *Um* Carmichael."

Fire lit behind her eyes, but he slammed the door before any retort could be made.

His sister had really screwed up this time. Question was, how bad?

Part of him didn't even want to know the answer to that.

CHAPTER FOUR

Hunter could hear a pin drop if he strained hard enough.

All of the men gaped at him as he told them the details of what had happened last night. When he finished, no one talked. No one. He could hear them breathing it was so quiet.

"That's some funny shit," Roc finally said, and burst out laughing.

"Dude," Blade admonished with a chuckle. That only served to get the other guys snickering.

"I can't believe y'all are laughing at me," Hunter said with a huff. "This could be serious."

"Yes," Bear said. "It could be. I think what Roc meant was that it's funny how quickly your sister assumed things."

"Hell, if the government was that on, they'd never need us," Brody added.

"Hey, the government knows what they're doing," Gauge said, frowning.

"Spoken like a true FBI agent," Roc muttered, all trace of humor gone. "The government doesn't know the difference between its ass and a hole in the ground. If it did, they wouldn't have so many dirty fucking people working for them."

"Not all agents are bad," Gauge said, shoulders back. But Hunter couldn't agree with him. Truth was, they were still weeding out the bad apples. No one was sure just how far the Collins crime family reach had been, and they had nearly two decades worth of digging still to do. Some of the agents in their pocket would have retired by now and not be a direct threat, but there were still some who worked for the feds that were deeply entrenched in the criminal life. It was one of the many reasons the Bang Shift was allowed to remain operable. Like it or not, the feds needed them.

At least while they cleaned house. Who knew beyond that?

"Maybe not the prized newbie," Roc added, crossing his arms.

"Fuck you, man. I've been with the FBI for years, and I've been at this garage for years. I'm not a fucking newbie."

"Cut it out, you two," Bear said, shaking his head. "We don't have time to go down that road right now. Let's figure out what we need to do about Hunter's sister and her friend. All that other crap can wait. It sure as hell isn't going anywhere." He looked at Hunter then. "What's your take on this?"

He'd been thinking about that on the way here, and he still didn't have a clear answer. "Don't know. It could be some little prick who was pissed, got drunk, and acted out. Don't make it right. Don't make it serious either." He shrugged.

"Or whoever took a slugger to that car could've drowned kittens growing up and is on a one-way path to becoming a serial killer," Blade said and pursed his lips. "Tough call."

"We don't have enough to go on," Brody said, sitting up straighter.

"Agreed." Bear nodded.

"We need that car," Roc said, adding something useful for the first time.

Gauge was already typing on his laptop. "Sheriff's office wouldn't have the means to deal with it. It'd be at the state's crime lab." After several more keystrokes, he said, "Yep. Checked in this morning, along with the evidence gathered at the scene."

Of course it was Gauge's FBI clearance and the latest government technology that allowed him to find that out, but the guy was too good of a person to make a petty comment about that.

"We need the results of that."

"And we need the car, so we can fix it," Hunter said without hesitation.

"Why?" Blade asked slowly.

"Because." He didn't have an excuse.

"Gauge," Bear said when Hunter didn't add anything else. "Keep watch on the chain of evidence and snag a copy. I'll call our contact with the feds and get an official copy of those results. Maybe we can get the big dogs on it and get a rush on the findings."

"Done," Gauge said with a short nod.

"And if they won't give them to us?" Hunter asked.

"I'll snag them anyway," Gauge said matter-of-factly without looking up.

"Brody, you stick with Xan. I don't think this is connected to her ex's family, but we can't be too careful.

Besides, I don't want her getting wind and worrying about anything."

"Don't even have to ask," Brody said. "I'll reach out to Jack Parsons. See if he can help."

"Good idea," Bear said.

"Well, those were the easy decisions. What are we gonna do about the girls?" Roc asked, eyebrow raised.

"They're here now. What does it hurt if they stay a few days? We might be able to get some preliminary news before they'd have to go back anyway. If anyone asks, your sister is here visiting with a friend. No big deal," Bear said.

It was a very big deal. His sister he could handle, but Maya? "The friend can't stay with me."

"Why not?" Blade asked, frowning. Then he slowly smiled. "Is she cute?"

"That doesn't have anything to do with it."

"That's a 'no' on the cuteness and an 'oh, baby' on the hotness." Blade wagged his eyebrows.

"Knock it off," Hunter said. "Her parents don't know she's here. If she misses classes, the school will probably notify them. She should either go home and face the music of her bad taste in boys, or go back to school and let the cops there deal with her."

"That why you want to fix her car? Because her parents don't know about it?" Bear asked.

"No," he said too quickly. Shit, that would have been a great excuse. "My sister rides around with her a lot, and I want to make sure she's taken care of."

"Who? Maya or your sister?" Roc asked.

"My sister, you asshole."

"Seems like a flimsy excuse to sink thousands of dollars into some broad's ride."

"Back the hell off, Roc," Hunter seethed.

"Jake Oberman—the boyfriend, ex, whatever—has already been picked up for questioning," Gauge said, breaking the tension. Hunter's head whipped around to find Gauge staring at his computer.

"That's good, right?" he asked.

"Yeah, er, no," Gauge said, frowning. "He was released. Not enough evidence. Oh shit."

"What?" Bear asked.

"He lawyered up. Bruce Cohen." The look Gauge gave him left a knot in his stomach. Before he could ask why that mattered, Gauge continued. "Cohen represents a lot of powerful people. A lot of *dirty* people. He's got connections all over the world. If he's in Jake's pocket, that kid could be really bad news."

"How bad?" Brody asked.

Gauge shrugged. "Don't know. Cohen's in it for the money, and there are a lot of rich criminals out there that use his services. We'd have to investigate them all to find a link. If there even is one."

"Does he represent anybody in the mafia?" Brody asked, his body becoming more rigid by each passing second.

"Oh, yeah," Gauge said. "Not sure if he reps anybody in Collins syndicate, but I wouldn't be surprised to find some connections, even if they're just minor.

Bear grunted. "That changes things." He looked at Hunter. "Maya's not going anywhere until we can ensure her safety. We'll have one of our people with the feds make contact with her parents. Tell them she's been selected for some D.C. trip. They'll contact the school, too, so she doesn't lose credit. She'll have to do her work, but she can do it remotely until we get to the bottom of this."

"What about my sister? They'll have to talk to the school about her, too."

"Actually, I was thinking something else for her."

"What?"

"You're not going to like it."

Hunter's jaw ticked. "What?"

Instead of answering him, Bear looked to Gauge. "Can we get an agent that resembles Maya?"

"Why?" Gauge asked after several seconds. Hunter knew the other man's brain was churning, but he was too focused on his own thoughts to be concentrating on what other people could be thinking.

"Because we can send an agent back with Heather to make some public appearances, making it look like she's living life normally, not worried about what happened to her car while we look into this."

"No." Hunter jumped up. "Did you just suggest sending my sister out there unprotected—"

"She'd be with an agent—"

"And make her fend for herself? No fucking way, man."

"It's not a bad idea," Blade said softly.

"No."

"I'm with Hunter. If the mafia is anyway involved, she needs to stay far away," Brody added.

"Right," Hunter said, knowing that Brody only agreed because of what happened with Xan, but not caring about the reasoning.

"Anna Sue could do it. She's worked with us before, so she'd take a personal interest in the case," Gauge said.

"No."

"She doesn't really look like Maya," Blade said.

"Doesn't matter. She's a chameleon. You'd be surprised how much she can change her appearance. Besides, she wouldn't have to go to class or anything. Just show up at a coffee shop, restaurant, bar—"

"No. Why aren't y'all listening to me?"

"Because you're looking at this emotionally," Bear said.

"You're goddamn right I am." Hunter shoved his finger toward Bear then looked at the rest of the room. "Y'all are talking about putting my sister on a case. She is inexperienced at best and a drama queen at worst. No way, no how, no. No. No. It's ridiculous to even consider."

"Bro, we're not talking about putting her in harm's way. Think about it. If neither of the girls are in town, Jake will know they're hiding. If he thinks the police questioned him and the girls are going around town as if nothing is wrong, it'll be easier for us to flush him out," Blade said.

"We can ask for additional support."

"I'll go," Hunter said. "I can protect my sister better than anyone."

"That won't work. If you're brooding around, Jake will know something's up. It has to look like the girls are doing their regular thing."

Hunter's teeth hurt from grinding them so much. "Yeah, but won't he think it's weird that I'm *not* there if she's in danger?"

"Not if the girls hid what happened," Roc said, glancing up at him.

"It's a solid idea," Blade added.

The door chimed, alerting the men to a customer.

"We need to get back to work," Bear said. "We'll go over the specifics after we close."

He could go over whatever he wanted, but Hunter would be damned if he agreed to what Bear had suggested. It was fucking madness.

"Hello? Guys? Anyone back there?" a female called out.

"Well fuck me," Hunter breathed. "I told her to stay

put," he yelled before storming out of the meeting room and into the lobby. "What are you doing here?"

And no, Heather wasn't alone. Maya stood cowering behind her. Great. What the ever lovin' fuck? When she didn't respond right away, he opened his mouth to ask again, but he stopped when he heard footsteps behind him. The guys had followed and were now within earshot.

"My car's acting up," she finally said. "Figured I'd bring it over to have it worked on while we're in town."

A sound suspiciously like a groan came from one of the guys. He looked over his shoulder and quickly scanned their faces. Yes, he knew his sister was a looker. It had been a problem for him ever since their parents had died, but no way was he going to tolerate one of his bros getting any ideas. It was bad enough he had to deal with the idea of boys her own age.

With his deadly stare, he dared each and every one of them to fucking try something with his baby sister. Each guy looked as impassive as Brody, who he knew wouldn't be thinking anything impure about his little Heather.

When he faced her again, he pinned her with that same killer gaze. "I could've taken a look at the house. I know a thing or two about cars." He realized his tone was sarcastic, but he didn't care.

"Well, look at you, Heather. All grown up," Bear said. He nudged Hunter to the side and gave her a hug. Hunter had to fight the instinct to rip his boss's arm off her. Deep down, he knew the man wouldn't try anything. Of course, Hunter had a problem right at this moment with rational thought. "We'd be happy to take a look at your car."

"You can't leave it here. I didn't drive my truck," Hunter said, shutting his eyes. Without a way home, the girls would have to hang around the shop.

"Why don't you pull it into the third bay over there? Roc can take a look at it."

"It'd be my pleasure," he said with a wink.

Hunter wanted to knock his ass out. Partly because of his co-worker's obvious flirting and partly because of his irritation that no one would listen to him.

"Will do," she said brightly, and tugged on Maya. "Let's go."

Hunter sighed, knowing it wasn't possible to change his sister's mind. Once the girls were back in the parking lot and Roc had a-little-too-eagerly gone into the bay, Bear turned to the remaining men.

"I don't want to pull rank, but I will if you don't get your head clear. Hell, you can't even stand one of your friends being around your sister without going all protective brother on us. No way can you guard her and effectively investigate."

"She. Is. My. Sister. Would you send Roxie out like that?"

The room was suddenly very quiet.

Hunter knew it was a low blow, bringing up Roxie, but he would do whatever was necessary to make sure his sister was safe.

Bear blinked. "What does that mean?"

"Cut the shit. You know what it means. You have a thing for her, and everybody knows it. So I'm asking you, would you put someone you cared about in the middle of danger like that?"

"I don't have a thing for Roxie. But even if I did, which I fucking don't, I'd do whatever was necessary to get the job done. Just like you're going to."

Hunter knew, in that moment, that Bear was one-hundred percent serious. Hunter needed to get on board or get overruled. Either way, it was fucking bullshit.

"What if I go?" Blade asked suddenly. "Just to keep an eye on things. Anna Sue can do her thing, and I'll be in the background. I'd watch your sister like a hawk, man." He looked at Bear. "I know we're swamped here, but we can push some projects back. If it'd make this easier on one of our own, then I think it's a no-brainer."

Hunter was in hell. Blade wasn't just a lady's man, he was the goddamn centerfold. How could Hunter agree to letting him guard his sister? He stared at the guy, wondering what he was supposed to do about this. He could either continue to fight his boss on this or he could give in and let the biggest flirt on their team watch his barely-legal sister's back. Yeah, that was an easy decision.

"Dude, I don't like the way you're looking at me," Blade said, hands up. "I might be a lady's man, but I know where the line is. And I know how to do my job."

As seconds ticked painfully by, he knew what the answer was going to have to be, and he didn't like it. Not one bit. Finally, he groaned with a slow nod. "Yeah, okay. Fine." He looked at Bear. "But I want updates from Anna. Jake so much as farts in the wrong direction, they're smoke. You feel me?"

"They'd be gone before they even get a chance to smell it."

"And if I think she's about to get a scratch on her, I'm out."

"That's fine," Bear said.

"I wasn't asking," Hunter reiterated.

Bear's gaze narrowed slightly, but he didn't fight Hunter on the comment.

"All right." He sighed.

Bear's shoulders dropped as if he'd been as tense as Hunter during this entire conversation. "Good. Now that *that's* settled, I'm going to make some calls, get Anna Sue here ASAP. We need to brief her, then get them back on the road." He craned his neck. "See anything on the car?" Bear called out.

"Battery cable's loose," Roc answered. "Tightening it now. She needs a tune-up." Hunter looked up in time to see Roc wink in their direction.

"Motherfucker," he breathed.

"He's just riling you up," Brody said. "Don't pay him any attention."

Easy for him to say.

"You know he's just a dick," Gauge added.

Rather than answering, Hunter said, "I need to talk to Heather."

"Yep. And Maya," Bear said.

Maya. He'd forgotten about her, the actual link to the trouble surrounding his sister, because he'd been so focused on who would keep his flesh and blood safe. "What's the plan with her?"

Bear's eyes grew infinitesimally. "She's your responsibility."

"What?" Hunter whispered heatedly.

Brody frowned at him. "Don't you think your sister will be more willing to play along if she knows her friend is in good hands? She brought her to you. She's only going to trust her care with you, dude. I'd take her to my place, but Scott goes through enough lotion as it is." He clapped Hunter on the back.

"You're the only one she knows," Bear added. "She's going to have to keep a low profile while she's here. I'd rather no one knew about her."

"Couldn't we put her in protective custody or something?" he asked, folding his arms. And he didn't *know* Maya. He'd only met her today, too.

"Get your sister to agree to that, and we'll make the calls," Bear said before he walked off.

Get his sister to agree? Right. Like that'd ever happen.

And Bear freakin' knew that, too.

Hunter was well and truly screwed. He didn't have any other choice but to go along with this plan. All of it. His sister would be shipped back to school at the earliest possible time, and he'd be stuck with a roommate for the foreseeable future. He looked across the garage and watched as Maya nervously chewed her thumbnail...and as his sister laughed carelessly at something Roc said. *Roc*.

Maybe the plan would be easier if he knew his sister could take something seriously for longer than a day.

And if that friend of hers wasn't so damn beautiful.

With one look at her, he knew she was going to be trouble.

Fuck, she already was.

CHAPTER FIVE

"You can't leave me here alone with him," Maya said to Heather. She knew she sounded desperate, but this wasn't the time for humility. She didn't know this man. At freaking all. She'd never met him before in her life, and now her friend happily went along with leaving her here alone with him.

"It'll be fine. Besides, did you see the guy he's sending me back with?" Heather said. "He's like a buff Spike from *Buffy*. A Buff Buffy's Spike." Heather giggled then.

"Is that all you care about?" Maya said heatedly as she grabbed the shirt that Heather was folding, repacking for her return trip. She'd unpacked after her brother left this afternoon, but Maya hadn't been ready to take that step, fruitlessly clinging onto a tiny shred of hope they wouldn't have to stay.

She should've been more specific with her wishes.

Their plans had quickly changed once they'd taken Heather's car to the shop, but not anything like she'd imagined.

If Friday night taught her anything, it should've been

how much things could change in a matter of hours. Maya wasn't sure how it happened so fast, but apparently, Hunter had called in some favors to look into the incident. For some reason, his people decided Heather could return to school, but Maya had to stay here.

At Hunter's house.

They hadn't been at the shop thirty minutes before being informed of this change of events. Hunter had borrowed one of the other guys' trucks to bring them back to the house—his house—with orders for Heather to be ready to leave this evening, and for Maya to make herself at home.

Yeah, right.

Why they were doing this, she had no idea. It made no sense to her. Of course, Heather didn't have anything to do with Jake. The two of them rarely saw each other; they hardly acknowledged the other when in the same room. She'd be surprised if Jake could even pick Heather out of a group of people. Maybe that was why Hunter agreed to his sister returning to campus.

"It's not all I care about," Heather finally said. "Besides, he's old."

"He's older than your brother."

"You think?" she asked, her head tilting to the side. Then she said, "Eww, on my brother, though."

"Really?"

Heather sighed, yanked her shirt back from Maya, and shoved it in her bag. "Chill out. I'm not really interested in Blade. Cool name, though," she added. "He's easy on the eyes,. So what if I'm making the best of a bad situation?"

"A totally messed up situation."

"Right. You should work on your adapting skills."

"My adapting skills are perfect."

Heather gave her a get-real look. "Fine, we need help,

but can you blame me? We left Texas to get away from danger and not only are you going back into it, but you're leaving me in an unfamiliar place."

Heather tugged on Maya's arm, and they sat on the edge of the bed. "You're scared. I get that. But my brother can help if you let him."

Maya looked up at the ceiling as she muttered, "What choice do I have?"

"Plenty, but they're all shittier than this one."

Pounding on the bedroom door made them both jump.

"Anna Sue is here. Shake a leg," Hunter said from the other side.

"Shake a leg?" Maya repeated, frowning at Heather.

"Welcome to Arkansas." She smiled. "You've already gotten the dime tour."

"I want my money back," Maya said, deadpan.

Bang. Bang. Bang. "Now, girls. I said, shake a leg!"

Heather jumped up, but Maya couldn't help but sneer at the door and the bossy man behind it.

"Let's go," Heather whispered as she slung her bag over her shoulder.

Maya stood up and followed her friend out of the room and down the hall. In the living room standing beside Hunter was Blade and what had to be lady who'd be impersonating her.

"This will never work," Maya said, her heart suddenly racing with the doom of impossibility. "She looks nothing like me."

"No offense, sweetie, but it's nothing a wig and some fake nails won't fix." She stepped up to her and stuck her hand out. "Anna Sue Fisher."

Maya shook the other woman's hand, and said, almost

panicked, "There's no telling what he'll do if he figures this out."

Anna Sue leaned closer and said just low enough for Maya to hear, "He'll beg for mercy." Then she straightened up and added, "I guess he can never know then." Anna Sue winked at her and stepped away.

Hunter had Heather to the side, whispering something to her. He looked very serious, and she looked like she was blowing off whatever he was telling her. Maya could feel the frustration pouring off him. After several minutes, he pulled her into his arms and hugged her.

"Be careful. And please listen to them."

"I will, Bubba."

Blade clapped his hands. "Let's hit the road."

Maya started to follow them out, but Hunter lifted a hand to stop her. "You, stay here."

She gaped at him, wanting to smart off about telling her what to do, but the look of pure determination told her he'd physically make sure she did what he wanted.

She couldn't think about what exactly that meant because if she dwelled on it, she'd hate the idea even more.

"Fine, I'm going to bed."

He opened his mouth as if he was going to say something, but the man had another thing coming if he thought she'd blindly fallow any order given.

Maya walked down the hall and to the guest room where they'd put her things before heading to the garage. She wasn't sleepy. She was too keyed up for that, but she wasn't hanging around here and be forced to talk to Hunter just yet. She needed time to process. Everything.

She had so much stuff to wade through, she didn't even know where to start.

She shut the door and walked to the window just in

time to watch as the SUV carrying Heather drive away, kicking up dirt and gravel behind it.

As she turned to walk away, she caught a glimpse of Hunter standing on the porch, facing the retreating car, but it almost looked as if his gaze was cut in Maya's direction, watching her instead.

It was dark, though. Surely she was seeing things.

CHAPTER SIX

Two. *Two* nights now Maya hadn't gotten any sleep. Friday night she'd been in too much shock about what Jake had done to get any rest. Last night, she'd not only been too overwhelmed with everything, but the strange bed didn't help matters. God, she was so tired.

After she'd thought about it some more in the wee hours of the morning, she'd been appreciative Hunter had agreed to help, though she wasn't sure what had made him change his mind. He'd been ready to kick her out of the house as soon as the girls had gotten there. The biggest reason she told herself not to complain about his one-eighty had nothing to do with him specifically and everything to do with her parents. With his help, she wouldn't have to tell them what had happened.

At least not yet.

She knew she couldn't keep it from them forever. Last night, she'd slowly realized that keeping them in the dark completely wouldn't work—because no way did she have the money to fix her car. Plus, since there was a police report, they'd probably contact her dad. His name was on the title, after all.

And his insurance company would probably get wind of it too.

Thinking she could work this out all on her own had been a crazy idea. *Stupid. Stupid. Stupid.* Another example of how naive she really was. That or how horribly she handled stressful situations.

But she wasn't completely nuts. No way could she tell her parents the truth. At least this bought her some time to come up with a plausible reason for what had happened, stopping her parents from pulling her out of school, and locking her in their basement for the next ten years like she thought they secretly wanted. Really. They had a basement, and it was finished. She's been told on several occasions she could live quite comfortably in it.

No thanks. She'd rather stay out from her under her parents' thumbs. If that meant she had to seek Hunter's help, she'd do it. Grudgingly.

After she stopped fretting about her parents, her busy brain jumped to another topic—wondering what the heck happened to make Jake snap. She had zero answers there, which ended up being all too much to ponder. Her parents. Jake. Jake. Her parents. Who could sleep with that many questions running around?

Granted, it'd been dark when Heather left, so it wasn't as if she'd had much time to unwind. After fleeing to her temporary bedroom, Maya had decided to take a quick shower to help her unwind before going to bed.

In Hunter's house.

Where she'd be staying for the foreseeable future.

She'd still been awake when he finally came back inside well after midnight. If she hadn't been, she would've woken up when the door to her room squeaked several minutes later. She'd lie there, frozen, wondering what he was doing as he'd obviously stood in the doorway, looking at her, but he hadn't stayed long enough for her to actually form a question. Not that she would've asked.

She'd been pretending to sleep, after all, hoping the real thing would happen any second.

She'd been wrong.

A sound coming from down the hall startled her and she jolted up.

He was up.

Hunter.

The only other person around for, probably miles.

She didn't know what to make of him. Oh, he was hot, but he was everything she'd ever envisioned a bad boy being, and not one like Jake. Hunter was genuine. Tall, built, attitude, and military.

Special ops. He was probably a member of a SEALs team or something. She knew those guys were bad to the bone. There were all kinds of books written about them. His name fit him. He probably *hunted* and took out enemy targets without breaking a sweat. Gun in one hand, sandwich in the other. Just another day for the sexy killer.

"You up?" he asked as he knocked on her door. She gasped. How the heck did he get down the hall without her hearing his approach? He was huge, for crying out loud. The old floor should've squeaked like the door had last night.

They probably taught that stealthy stuff in SEALs school.

"I'm awake. Not up," she called, figuring if she didn't answer, he'd come in.

"Shake a leg. Biscuits're in the oven."

"O-kay," she said slowly, not knowing how else to respond.

A thud sounded on the other side, so she tossed the warm blanket off in case it was a sign he was about to come in to make sure she was complying. No way did she want to give the big baddy a reason to be irritated with her.

When the door didn't creak, she figured he wasn't going to barge in. Hopefully, he silently went back the way he'd come.

Jeez, I'm not ready to deal with him just yet, she thought as her legs dangled over the side. How could she be? So much had happened in such a short amount of time. She looked around the sparsely decorated room and decided she'd take her time getting ready. Biscuits could wait.

So could Hunter, the hunting SEAL.

She slid off the bed and rummaged in her suitcase. Everything seemed too revealing. Jeans were meant to be tight. Shirts were low cut. She never felt as if she'd dressed provocatively before, but now everything screamed "Slutty McSlutster." She almost squealed when she saw her sweats underneath another set of PJs. Those would work. In fact, she should start wearing stuff like that all the time. No need to draw the attention of more jerks. When it was time for her to move on, she'd find her a nice, unassuming hipster who'd appreciate a more homely wardrobe.

Feeling better about her future plans, she took her time changing. Once she was covered, she dug in the side pocket for her toothbrush. Her hand brushed against something, making her frown, and she pulled it out.

The note left in her car.

Her damaged car.

On Friday night.

She began to shake as she stared at the crumpled paper.

She hadn't forgotten about it, but the physical reminder was too much, too soon.

Not only a painful reminder of the other night, but of all the crap Jake had put her through.

How had she ever thought him decent? Even in the beginning, she should have seen the signs. Should've known better than to trust a man like him.

Walking toward the bed, she began to stretch the note out. She spread it across her pillow to smooth it some more. When she'd gotten it as even as she could, she read the note again. Why? Because maybe the harsh proof would keep her from doing anything stupid—like falling for a jerk —again.

The message was clear. Very clear, and Maya couldn't help the tear that formed in her eye.

She swiped it away, muttering, "It doesn't matter."

What mattered was making sure she never fell victim to a man like that again. Period.

She folded the note, put it back in her suitcase—saving it in case she ever needed another reminder—and took a deep, cleansing breath before grabbing her toothbrush to finish getting ready. She might even take an extra step to make sure the man down the hall wouldn't try anything with her, ensuring she'd succeed with keeping all bad boys out of her personal life. Maybe.

She'd have to hurry, though.

Biscuits awaited.

———

HUNTER REACHED into the hot oven and grabbed the biscuits, leaving the iron skillet in there until it cooled.

Why was he even cooking breakfast? There was a diner a few miles down the road.

Because Maya can't be seen around town, and you don't have any cereal. It was the same thing he'd repeated to himself until he grabbed the frozen biscuits and turned on the oven.

This was a babysitting job. And by baby, he didn't mean the hot, *oh-baby*-baby, as Blade had joked. Though Maya's body was killer and her timid demeanor only added to her sexiness. Still, the assignment amounted to nothing more than watching her as if she were a toddler. Or worse, a prisoner. He knew it. He fucking knew it, but he couldn't do anything about it. If she wasn't here, he'd be tempted to catch the next flight to Dallas and keep an eye on his sister. Bear probably knew that, which was why he'd given him the crap excuse about Maya knowing him best, effectively ending any chance Hunter had at refusing this job.

Though his sister had sure-as-shit laid it on thick after she'd been brought up to speed on the plan, saying he had to protect her friend, for her. For *her*. Didn't matter in what kind of hard place it put Hunter.

And that hadn't been the only thing hard. Fuck. His libido acted as if he had never been inside a woman when he was around Maya. Even last night, as she pretended to sleep, just the scent of her thickened the air and had him sporting wood. He'd have called her out on her little possum routine if he hadn't feared what she had on underneath that blanket. He hadn't been sure if he could control himself had she been wearing anything skimpy. Or worse...nothing at all.

Which was insane. He was a professional.

Maya was his sister's friend.

His ward for God knew how long.

And she was way too young for him. He wasn't into younger women. If anything, he preferred the older, more experienced females. The ones who knew how to please a man without any guidance. They saw a hard cock and got busy. Yeah, he loved that.

Young and innocent? That wasn't his style. Not that he knew if she was truly innocent in the sexual department. And didn't *that* just pique his interest a little too much? He acted like a horny teenager, getting hard just being around a woman. He'd grown out of that phase fifteen years ago.

It had to stop. This wasn't like him. He was always easy-going, even around the ladies, but since yesterday, he'd felt an edge creep in, one he knew if he didn't control would make it harder to hide the hardness in him he'd always kept under wraps. He wouldn't let one little chick get under his skin. He'd make sure of it.

The sooner he could get the goods on Jake Oberman, the sooner he could send Maya back to school.

And he could forget about her.

Not to mention, his sister would be out of this mess. Christ, he would've thought Heather would be the one to commandeer his thoughts, not the girl down the hall.

The only saving grace right now was knowing his sister was in capable hands. Anna Sue had proven herself when shit hit the fan before, and he'd trusted Blade with his own back more times than he could count. Yeah, he knew Heather would be okay. It wouldn't stop him from worrying, though. After their dad died in the motorcycle accident, Hunter had taken on the role of father in addition to brother. He'd been young, but he'd still felt the need to watch over the females and provide for them. That desire had been the driving force for him when he'd dabbled in a life of crime—the fastest way to make big bucks. He was just glad he'd turned his life around before his mother had died too. Now both of their parents were gone. Heather was all he had left.

And Maya was her friend. A friend he'd sworn to protect. Damn Heather and her big, brown eyes. Like a lost puppy, she was, when she worked that stare. He'd practically jumped at the chance to play warden. Okay, not really, but it sure as hell felt like he'd been all too agreeable. His sister would drive him mad one day, he was sure of it.

He heard Maya enter and pushed all thoughts of Heather and all inappropriate thoughts of his temporary roommate away. He was making himself crazy with them anyway.

"Want jelly?" he asked after she'd moved a chair at the table, probably sitting down.

"Oh my gosh. I tiptoed. How did you know—never mind. Not supposed to ask," she muttered at the end.

He rolled his eyes as he stepped to the fridge, keeping his back to her. He retrieved two kinds of jellies and butter. When he turned to the table, he glanced at her as he put the items down.

And burst out laughing.

"What?"

He shook his head and turned away to grab the two plates of biscuits and silverware he'd pulled out earlier. "Nothing," he said, still smiling as he sat and pushed her plate toward her clasped hands.

She reached for a butter knife, and he looked up. Her cheeks were a delectable pink. What was she thinking right now? Had he embarrassed her? His smile fell as guilt crept in. That had to be it. He'd just laughed at her. Or so she probably thought.

"I'm sorry." He shoved half a biscuit in his mouth before

he could say more. What could he say? She had twisted her hair into a messy ponytail, wore oversized sweatpants, and had zit medicine spread across her face. It looked as if she was trying *not* to look attractive. He'd laughed, not because of the shocking difference, but because her attempt had been futile. She could be wearing a burlap sack and still be fucking gorgeous.

Okay, maybe he had laughed at her, but not for any reason she could've come up with.

"The Clearasil's a bit much, huh?" she asked as she rubbed some of it in, making it disappear into her skin. Then she reached for the butter.

"Nah. Just wasn't expecting it." He shrugged, deciding it was best not to say too much. He ate the rest of his biscuit as he forced his mind onto something other than her looks. She wasn't making it easy, especially after catching him off guard with her appearance, but he gritted his teeth and forged ahead. She was an assignment. Period. He had a job to do, and the first thing that came to him was that he needed information from her. She was here for a reason, and there was no time like the present to pump her for intel. "Tell me about Oberman."

"Huh?" Her hand stopped, knife in mid-air.

"Your ex," he said, raising an eyebrow at her.

"Um, Heather—I—we told you what happened---"

"I know what happened Friday," he said, shaking his head. "I mean, tell me about him. I need to know *all* about him."

"I, er, well, there's not much to say. He's a bouncer at a nightclub." She licked the side of her thumb, and he forced himself not to watch her tongue slipping out. Another thought startled him, making it easier to briefly ignore her sexual appeal.

"The same place you were at Friday night?" Jesus, surely she wouldn't willingly put herself around his place of business if she'd wanted away from him.

"No," she said slowly. "I might not be very street smart, but I'm not a complete idiot." She rolled her eyes and continued preparing her biscuit.

"Well, there's that," he said under his breath, but judging by her little harrumph, he hadn't said it as quietly as he'd intended. Then her comment fully registered. "What do you mean you're not very street smart?"

She shrugged, looking away. "My parents were protective."

"Strict?" he guessed.

She wrinkled her nose as she looked at him again. "No, not really. I mean, yeah, I couldn't do some of the things my friends did—like I didn't get a cell phone until I was sixteen." She smirked.

"What?" He half-smiled. "That's crazy talk right there."

"I know, right? Even then it was only because I got my license. I could do the social media thing from my laptop or tablet, so I wasn't living completely in the Dark Ages." She took a bite of her breakfast and cleared her throat as she put it down. "Where are the cups? I need some water."

He immediately stood. "Shit, sorry. I meant to get you a drink." After grabbing a cup, he opened the fridge. "I don't have much here." He looked over his shoulder. "But I do have O.J. That okay? At least then when you talk to Heather, you don't have to tell her I fed you bread and *water*. I'd really feel like a warden then." He winked. The joke had come easy. They always had.

But this was different. It *felt* different. The moment he'd winked, her face flushed and her pretty little lips formed a

perfect "O" of surprise. She was too expressive. Too innocent. And he'd flirted with her.

Fucking flirted.

Good job at staying professional. He turned around,
grabbed a glass, and poured the juice. The tension in the
room was palpable. The muscles in his back were getting
stiffer by the second. He could easily blame the crackling in
the air on the fact he hadn't gotten laid in a while, but it'd be
a lie. Not the getting laid part, but the other, dangerous part.
He could *feel* the interest wafting off her. It was there. She
wanted him. Some part of her did, at least.

He needed to get away. Right now.

Before he changed his mind, he slammed the glass on
the table in front of her. "There's something I need to take
care of. I'll be back." He pivoted, knowing he was being
abrupt all of a sudden, but not caring. The only thing that
mattered was his riding boots were by the back door, and
he'd be needing them.

"W-where are you going?"

He didn't look at her as he bent down to put on his
shoes. "Can't say. But don't try to leave. We've got plenty of
eyes."

"What?"

He straightened and turned, looking at her again. She
glanced around as if she was currently being watched. Her
vulnerability only added to her appeal, but he didn't correct
her thinking. He couldn't chance it. If he stayed a second
longer, he might do something he'd regret. Instead, he did
the only thing he could do. He rushed from the house as he
fished out his cell phone. Gauge's number beckoned him,
and he didn't hesitate to select it. His friend answered on
the second ring.

"What up, my brother?"

"Need you to watch the house for a few hours. Gotta run to the store," he lied.

"Maya going with you?"

"No," he said quickly. "She can't be seen around town," he added as he marched toward his motorcycle.

"Mmm-hmm. Sounds like you're running away."

"I fucking wish."

Gauge laughed. "Hasn't been twenty-four hours yet, bro. Figured you'd last longer than that."

"You comin' or not?" Hunter asked, not interested in his chain being yanked, and straddled his bike, itching to hit the road. He needed to ride, feel the wind, and do his best not to keep driving away.

"Yeah, heading out the door," Gauge said a little more seriously.

"Good. I'll be watching from down the road. Won't leave until I know you're here."

His buddy didn't respond right away, and then said, "She's pretty."

"Don't," he barked.

"All right, all right. You know how to stay detached. Think of her as just another job. She'll be out of your hair before you know it."

And still, it wouldn't be soon enough.

CHAPTER SEVEN

"Shit," Hunter yelled after banging his head on the fender of the car he'd been working on since he'd gotten to work early this morning. He wheeled himself out from under it with a hasty shove and wiped the sweat from his brow using the greasy rag he'd tucked into his pocket.

What a morning. Hell, weekend for that matter. What had started out like any other normal Saturday had turned to anything but normal when his sister called. Now he had a houseguest.

A beautiful one.

One he'd run from yesterday morning and had stayed away from until late into the night. Gauge hadn't given him any lip when he'd returned after midnight, just nodding at him when he drove by. A text a few seconds later had updated him that their charge had turned in and was sleeping soundly.

Hunter had taken the Pig Trail into the Ozarks, ridden those winding mountain roads into Northwest Arkansas, and had let the scenery push all thoughts of Maya and his unnaturally-sudden attraction to her from his mind. It had worked, too, until he'd gotten home. He'd felt the tension return, seeping into his bones, the moment he'd walked into his house. It had taken every ounce of willpower not to look into her room and watch her sleep. He'd been thankful Gauge had informed him of her status. Otherwise, he'd have been obligated to physically check for himself.

He hadn't needed the temptation.

Still didn't, which was why he'd left early this morning to come into the garage. He'd already wasted a tank of gas avoiding her. At least here he could be productive and earn money, rather than blow it on fuel. Only reason he'd been able to get away with this little break was because Bear had been meeting with their federal contacts this morning about Maya's ex. He'd taken Gauge with him since that dude was part of the fed family. Jack Parsons had even been there.

"You okay, man?" Brody asked from the other bay as he wiped his hands on his jeans. Again. He hadn't touched the truck that had been lifted. Why he kept rubbing his clean hands on his practically dryer-fresh clothes, Hunter didn't know, but it was obvious the guy was acting weird. It was probably something about Xan or Scott. Domestic stuff.

He hadn't been given any specifics, though.

His grunt was the only response he provided as he rolled to a tool station and leaned against it. He rubbed his throbbing noggin where he'd made contact with the under-belly of a wheel well. Maybe he should check in on Heather. That'd take his mind off Maya while still working on the case.

"Wouldn't have happened if you were at the house," Roc said as he leaned around the '55 he'd claimed an hour ago. Hunter flipped him off before turning away. He didn't care what Roc thought. The man did what he needed to get by, but he was still out for number one.

Should Hunter have stayed home to watch Maya? Probably. She was his responsibility. If he hadn't known Bear wouldn't be at the shop, he wouldn't have chanced coming in. No way. The only thing *that* would've accomplished was his ass getting handed to him by his boss. Besides, no one knew Maya was in this little town. She had no connection to Hunter. But he wasn't completely ignoring his duties. He had an obligation, and he wouldn't have left if he didn't think she was completely safe. He'd turned on his alarm, so he'd know if Maya so much as opened a window, and that only covered one part of his high-tech system. He had cameras all over his property and was notified of any movement made. He'd been able to describe every deer and squirrel within a two-mile radius until he changed some of the settings. Now squirrels were omitted, but he'd rather be alerted to a buck than chance of not being notified of any human activity.

And yeah, it came in handy during hunting season, too.

Maya wasn't going anywhere without him knowing, nor was anybody coming anywhere near her. He'd never had a problem with his setup, but Bear wouldn't see it the same way. Thankfully, Hunter knew his boss well enough to know he'd check in before heading back. That'd give him time to scratch pavement.

With his phone in sight, he reached for it.

"Tell that hot-ass sister of yours I said hi," Roc said, practically growling.

Hunter's head snapped around. "The fuck did you say?"

Roc's glare was nothing but taunting.

Hunter leapt to his feet. "You mother—"

"Ah hell," Brody rumbled and jumped in front of him. "Not again, man. You know how he is. He only does that shit to get under your skin."

"I prefer to be on top, but I'd be willing to be under Heather."

Hunter pointed at Roc over Brody's shoulder. "That's not happening."

"Scared she won't know how to handle a real man after living all these years with you?"

"You don't know when to shut up, do you?" Brody asked, exasperated.

"Stay the hell away from my sister."

The door connecting the lobby to the garage slammed. Hunter's gaze cut toward it, not willing to relax his squared-off stance in case Roc came at him.

He shouldn't have looked.

"What in God's name are you doing here?" Bear asked. *Busted.*

"'S all right," Brody said, turning as if to defend Hunter from Bear instead of blocking Roc from Hunter. "Called Willis. He's been shadowing Hunter's place."

"You called Flint?" Bear asked, frowning.

"Yeah, Roxie was at the house this morning when Roc texted me 'bout Hunter being at the garage. Said Flint's days off were Monday and Tuesday and he could help."

Bear rubbed his face as he took in the information.

Hunter wasn't as willing to let it digest. "You told Xan *and* Roxie about Maya?" he yelled as he faced his colleague. Bad enough Brody had said something to his woman about a job—regardless if it wasn't one they'd been specifically hired for—but he told Roxie? That woman loved to gossip and get up in everybody's business.

"Better back down. You know that's not how I roll. Message came in while we were all at the table. Said you and Gauge were busy and I needed to hightail it over to Hunter's to watch the place. Roxie offered to message her cousin. He hasn't done us wrong—"

"He's a cop," Roc said, moving away from the '55 and heading toward the other guys. Yes, Flint Willis was the sheriff around here, but the Bang Shift crew did their best to stay off the local police's radar. When it was unavoidable, the feds stepped in. The guys were lucky the local boys weren't all up in their business. If there were other factions out there like theirs, he doubted those arrangements were as accommodating.

But Flint Willis wasn't just an officer. He also happened to be Bear's old hunting buddy and the closest thing he had to a best friend until some fall out happened between the two of them a year or two ago. Bear chose to avoid that man whenever possible, and Brody knew that.

They all did.

Hunter took a deep breath, immediately feeling bad for yelling at Brody. Why had he acted out like that? He knew Brody understood the score. Then again, no mission had ever been so personal to him.

Because of his sister. That was it. No other personal connection.

Bear ignored Roc's outburst and any broken connections he had to the man, instead asking, "What was Roxie doing at your place so early this morning?"

No one was surprised Bear turned his inquisition to Roxie at the mention of her name. The man probably hadn't realized he'd done it, and none of them would call him out on it. Hunter's slip the other day was a big, unspoken no-no.

Brody rubbed his clean hands on his pants again. "Xan wanted to talk to her."

"Dude, what's up? You could crawl the walls you're so spastic," Hunter asked Brody, unable to keep the question inside anymore.

The big, blond man looked at him before training his gaze on each of the other men, taking his time before he replied. Hunter couldn't be sure, but the man almost looked scared, which didn't make any sense. Brody was one of the biggest badasses he knew. Hunter had seen him face danger head-on without batting an eyelash. He was as tough as they came. The toughest. Besides himself, of course.

"Xan and I...we're getting married."

Hunter stilled. They all seemed to have frozen. But after a moment of quiet, cheers erupted.

"'Bout time you made an honest woman outta her," Bear said, clapping Brody on the shoulder.

"Who cares about that?" Roc said, smiling. "When're we hitting the titty bar?" Brody shoved him, and he chuckled on his way back to the classic car he'd claimed.

"Dude, getting hitched," Hunter said, plastering a smile on his face. This was something his friend wanted to celebrate and smiling was the norm, though he felt anything but joy on the inside. Marriage. It was something he'd never get to experience. Maybe in another life things would've been different, but his past aside, he didn't feel right bringing a woman into all this. He never knew when he'd have to leave on assignment.

Or if he'd return.

They'd been lucky the last couple of years, but before that they were gone more often than not. With the government so focused on the Middle East, there hadn't been as great a need for their services stateside, nor in areas where wars were not being waged. That could change any second. A politician could get a wild hair up his ass and the next thing Hunter knew, he'd be shipped off to some godforsaken hellhole.

"If I can find happiness, anybody can," Brody said, as if he'd read Hunter's mind.

"Leave the sappy stuff to Hallmark." He smirked. "We all know your situation is different." Xan had been in hiding from her ex and his family. She'd been used to a life on the run and exposed to unimaginable crime. She was one tough cookie.

"It doesn't have—"

"Gonna stop you there," Hunter chided gently as he put his hands on Brody's shoulders. "This is about you and your woman. Happy for you. Really."

And in that second, a part of him meant it.

"Thanks, man."

Stepping back, Hunter said, "Now, I want to call my sister and should probably head back to the house before Bear shakes off the mention of Roxie's name and realizes he hasn't renamed me yet."

Brody chuckled and glanced over his shoulder. "By the glaze in his eyes, I'd say you have about seven more minutes."

"I only need two." He winked before turning around. He slipped out the door while Bear stood, arms crossed, staring at a two-year old calendar on the wall. The model was hot, so none of the guys ever bothered taking it down.

Bear hadn't been looking that far up, though. Hunter could tell whatever his boss was looking at, he wasn't actually seeing. Didn't matter. Bear and his not-so-secret fascination with Roxie wasn't any of Hunter's business.

He straddled his bike and pulled out his phone. First, he'd check in with his sister. Then he'd go back home.

He had a feeling there would be no more breaks from Maya, no matter how much temptation she'd be for him. His only reprieve was ending, and there wasn't anything he could do about it.

CHAPTER EIGHT

"I'M BORED," Maya said to Heather as they chatted over the phone, knowing she sounded like a whiny baby, but not able to care. "It's only been like a week, and I don't know how much longer I can stand this."

Heather snorted. "It's been four days. Hardly a week."

Might as well have been an eternity. There was only so much exercising a girl could do before she couldn't take the screaming muscles anymore. She'd worked out three times yesterday—once after she'd woken up, finding herself alone —and two more times after Hunter came grumbling back in toting some groceries, only to close himself in his bedroom. A few times, she'd heard the radio blaring in there, and she'd considered going outside for a run, but anytime she'd touch the doorknob, he'd appear out of nowhere. He wouldn't say anything. Just stare, waiting for her to do something. She was pretty sure the look was meant to intimidate her, but all she saw was heat in his sexy eyes.

She apparently hadn't learned her lesson about bad boys because every time she looked at Hunter, she wanted to...she didn't know. She just wanted.

So, yeah, she had already worked out twice today, trying to keep her mind off her captor. Because that was what he was. After returning yesterday, he hadn't left again. He was here.

He was everywhere.

He was nowhere.

An enigma. Always out of her sight unless she considered stepping out of the house.

"Same difference."

"Is not." Then Heather said, "O-M-G. Is my brother being a punk?"

"I don't want to talk about him."

"He is. Jeez. I'm sorry. I was worried about that when they made you stay back. But I figured he'd be too busy looking into Jake."

Maya sighed. "I don't want to talk about him either." He was the reason she was in the mess to begin with.

"Well, maybe you'd like to know he hasn't tried anything. I saw him on campus, and he didn't even acknowledge me. You know how he is; if he's mad about something, he's gonna make sure you know it. Doesn't care how much of an ass it makes him look. So, you know, maybe his daddy talked some sense into him, and he's gonna be chill now."

"Don't see it being that easy." But if that was the case, she could go back to school. Get away from Hunter. Get back to normalcy. Hell, she didn't even like exercising. "How long do you think we'll have to wait before I get the all-clear?"

"Not sure." Heather's voice dipped lower. "I heard Blade talking to Anna about tailing him. I didn't get much more than that. I sorta got caught eavesdropping."

"Of course you did," Maya said sarcastically. "Incognito isn't your style."

"Oh, shut up. It's not like it doesn't involve me. I have a right to know."

"Because you are the one stuck in a cabin in the woods."

"C'mon. It's not a cabin. Civilization isn't that far away. Fast Internet connection, too, not dial-up."

"Do they even make dial-up anymore? Might as well start selling me on the fact that he has one of those new fangled *microwaves* everyone's talking about. Give me a break."

Heather snickered. "You have your phone and laptop—"

"I have a *burner* phone, whatever the hell that is, not my phone. And your brother took my laptop away that first night and did something to it."

"Okay, okay, you've got cabin—"

"I swear to God, if you say I have *cabin fever*, I will destroy your favorite skirt when I get back."

"Going stir crazy? That better?"

"Marginally," she muttered.

Heather huffed. "I know this isn't ideal, but please make the best of it. I'm going to feel really bad about taking you out there if I know you are just completely miserable."

"But I am," Maya groaned.

"Look, I'll talk to my brother and see if I can get some idea about how much longer they think you need to be sequestered."

"Thank you. I'd do it, but he's pretending I'm not even here." From the time he'd gotten home yesterday, she might as well be invisible, except for a few moments of catching him staring at her. It had taken less than a minute to realize the feelings in her stomach had been butterflies at his attention. Was it because he was looking at her at all or because he'd caught her off guard? She didn't know.

Heather was silent for several seconds before she asked, "Really?"

"Why do you sound so surprised? You were the one who always talked about how hard and dangerous your brother is," she said instead of divulging her thoughts. Hell, she didn't know what to think, and if those thoughts veered toward how sexy Hunter was, she got irritated and forced herself to stop.

"His job. You know, with the military. He takes work stuff seriously," she said, almost rambling. "But he always clowns around. Especially when things get a little hairy. And he's usually the one to step in and make someone feel comfortable in those situations. I'm just a little surprised he's not acting like himself is all."

"Your brother? A jokester?" Maya laughed. She found *that* hard to believe. Even when she caught him silently looking at her, there was no humor in his gaze. There was something there, something deeper, something she had no business trying to figure out. But light-heartedness was not it. There was also what little Heather had told her about him since becoming friends. Add to that what she'd found out about his military career on the way here, and yeah, Maya never envisioned him being the life of the party.

A knock startled her. She covered the phone and looked toward the door. "Yeah?"

Hunter cracked it open and peeked in. "I'm going for a run. Need to check some things around the perimeter. Stay put."

"Yes, sir," she drawled. Heat flared in his eyes before he cursed and slammed the door shut, leaving her staring at the painted wood. Her spine tingled at the fleeting look he'd given her, but the tingle was followed quickly by irritation. Why did he think he could just order her around?

"Hello?" Maya heard coming from her lap.

"Oops. Sorry. That was Mr. Happy, ordering me to stay like a good little puppy."

"I'll talk to him—"

"No. Last thing I need is for another man to think I'm weak. Just...let me know if you find anything out, okay?"

"You know I will."

They said their goodbyes, and Maya tossed the phone onto the bed once the call ended. What was she supposed to do now? She exhaled slowly as she considered her slim options. She'd logged into her classes this morning and finished those assignments, knowing she had to stay caught up. After all the crap with Jake had gone down, she'd thrown herself into school, working ahead in her classes, scouring over each syllabus and doing what she could. She couldn't depend on schoolwork to keep her distracted, now.

Reading was her go-to thing when she had extra time, but she'd re-read her book twice now—that would teach her not to delete them from her library when she got finished. If she read it again, she'd be able to recite it, so that was out.

She could exercise again, but the thought of doing another round of sit-ups and push-ups totally depressed her.

She gasped, sitting up straighter as an idea hit her. She could always go for a jog. *Hmmm.*

Outside.

Fresh air, new scenery. Yeah, she was liking that idea a lot. So what if Hunter had told her to stay put? She wasn't some lapdog. She was a person. She had free will. What crime had she committed to warrant this kind of treatment? None—that was what. Besides, it wasn't like she was leaving the property. And Hunter *was* still here.

She was totally going to do it.

After grabbing her sneakers, she quickly slipped them on and jumped up. She looked at the bedroom door and slowly opened it. She pushed away any feelings of guilt over not minding him away. He wasn't one of her parents, and she wasn't sneaking out to go to some party. She was well within her rights to do this. As she walked down the hall, she couldn't help but wonder how long it would take before Hunter realized she'd left the house. He seemed to have some weird sixth sense about that. When the backdoor came into view, only one thought came to her. *There's one way to find out.*

As if in a trance, she threw open the door and bolted down the back stairs. The cool air warmed by the sun's rays washed over her face, making her smile as she jogged a few steps. It was invigorating. She would never take the outside for granted again. Maybe she should take up this form of exercise when she got back to campus. *Let's not get hasty.* She smiled even wider. But as she turned the corner, she saw something that would've made her stop short if she wasn't so shocked.

Hunter, darting out of the trees, barreling toward her. The look on his face was one of panicked determination.

"What's wrong?" he roared right before he tackled her, rolling them to the ground against the side of the house.

She was too stunned to answer. The fact that his hard-as-steel body blanketing her hadn't even registered right away was proof of how shocked she was.

His panting breath bathed her neck, making it even harder for her to form words. If she opened her mouth, incoherent nonsense would spew. Or worse. She'd make some noise she knew would sound suspiciously like a moan.

Oh god, he was so big. The heat radiating off him was

making her weak. She grabbed his arms to steady herself. She was either going to pass out or the world was literally spinning—and faster than it was supposed it.

"Did you get some kind of threat?" She tried shifting, but couldn't. "Stay down," he whispered heatedly. "No alarms went off. No one should be past the fence line." He scanned the area. His neck corded as he gritted his teeth. It was one of the sexiest things she'd ever seen. Her heart raced, the air completely gone from her lungs.

Spots danced in front of her eyes as she tried to focus on him, realization dawning as to why her body reacted so strongly, at least partly. "Can't breathe," she wheezed. He was crushing her.

He cursed as he lifted a little. "Sorry, darlin'." The endearment rolled off his tongue as if without effort, and heat rushed to her face. She liked the way it sounded, him calling her that. Which was crazy. This was the South. She could've been an eighty-year-old grandma and he would've said the same thing. It wasn't something special to him. It shouldn't be to her.

"It's okay."

His gaze finally met hers. "I'm tracking zero threats. What happened? Why were you running?" he asked, still all business.

"I-I—" Crap. She hadn't considered what her running from the house would look like to him if he'd been watching the door. "Sorry," she said meekly. "I wanted some fresh air."

He moved again, the pressure of the rocky ground easing a little more. Her back and leg stung something fierce, but she couldn't bring herself to push him away. Not that she'd be able to do much good in that department. He was a wall and wouldn't be going anywhere unless he wanted.

That so shouldn't have turned her on.

She watched as the calculated look in his eyes slowly changed. *Oh shit.*

"You mean to tell me you ran from the house like it was on fire because you wanted to? I *told* you to stay put." He rolled off her, cussing up a storm, and then muttering words that were unintelligible.

A snotty retort was on the tip of her tongue, but the burning in her leg got stronger. When she opened her mouth, all she managed to utter...was a wince.

"What–*fuck.*" He jumped up. Before she could ask what his deal was, he scooped her into his arms.

"Ooph."

"You're bleeding." He carried her into the house while she twisted some, trying to see what he was talking about. "Your leg," he said, answering her silent question. How he managed to get up the stairs, through the door, and her deposited onto the bathroom counter without so much as another jostle, she didn't understand. But the moment he grabbed her inner thigh, she no longer cared about his superhuman abilities.

Or the fact that she was bleeding somewhere on her leg.

He pushed her knees farther apart and she suppressed a gasp as she gripped the edge of the counter. When he moved closer, she had to look up. The image of his head between her legs had blood rushing to other parts of her body, and she had to manually control the speed at which she breathed.

He moved, his arm brushing against her side before she heard the squeak of something and then water.

"I need to clean it. It might be deep."

His voice was smooth with apparent concentration, but all she could think about was how the word *deep* slipped off his tongue and all the other meanings that tiny word could signify.

Jesus, was it a thousand degrees in here? She was burning up. She was so attracted to this man. There was no denying what he did to her, how she reacted to him. She wanted him. His scent taunted her, making her wonder if he tasted just as good.

"W-where is it?" she asked, finding her voice.

The pause was palpable, and she squeezed her eyes shut, trying to shut him off from her senses. All that managed to do was heighten her hearing; his heavy breaths might as well have been screams.

"Here," he murmured, circling an area on her left inner thigh toward the back. She swallowed and nodded, not knowing why she bothered asking. Maybe she just wanted him to touch her there again.

When a cool cloth grazed her skin, she let out the gasp she'd swallowed earlier. "Cold." She smiled, looking down at him.

He glanced up from his task and smiled. He looked at her for several seconds longer than necessary before clearing his throat and looking down again. "Just a scratch. Must've caught it on a rock or something."

"So no trip to the E.R. then?" she quipped.

His lips tugged at the corner as if he was fighting a smile. "No. You're good."

"Always good when a man tells a woman that," she said softly.

His head snapped up.

Oh crap, why did she say that? What was wrong with her? It was bad enough she couldn't deny her body's reaction to him, but that didn't mean she should flirt with the man. With him standing between her legs. His hand on her bare skin. Body heat scorching the air.

"Maya," he breathed. His tongue darted out to wet his lips, and any will she pretended she possessed came crashing down. Her hand rose as if it had a mind of its own, and she stroked his stubble-roughened cheek. The sound that rumbled up from his chest set her core on fire. Rational thought? Gone. Nowhere was reason in this room. She leaned in instead of thinking about it. She could do nothing else. She watched his Adam's apple bob before her lips finally touched his. He moaned, angling his head. The heat of his mouth bathed hers. She had to stop herself from shoving her tongue down his throat and kissing him as if it was her first time and she had no skill whatsoever. But she wanted, needed to feel the wet heat of him.

She moaned as their noses bumped, a signal the kiss was milliseconds away from fully happening, and she wanted it more than her next breath.

But suddenly, Hunter jerked away from her.

His gaze darted to his watch right before a deafening sound screeched all around them.

What the hell?

Maya's hands flew to her ears, but before she could ask him anything—not thinking right then that he wouldn't be able to hear her—he pointed at her, then to the floor before putting his finger to his lips in the universal sign to keep quiet.

He eased back from her as he fiddled with his watch. Now that she really looked at it, though, it didn't look like a regular timepiece. It was digital with all kinds of blinking lights on it.

The sound stopped. Hunter slowly opened the door,

but before he left, he looked at her again. "Stay. I *fucking* mean it this time."

"What's going on?" she asked hurriedly.

"That was the alarm. Someone set it off. I'm going to kill whoever it is," he whispered as he left, though she wasn't sure if that last part was meant for her ears or not.

A new kind of adrenaline rushed through her. Gone was the excitement of feeling Hunter's lips against hers, replaced with something much starker.

She could be in danger. Like real danger. But battling that fear for dominion was another bleak possibility.

Hunter's instinct had been to protect her at all costs. Would he shoot first and ask questions later? Her naive, sheltered brain couldn't wrap around any of those thoughts.

Yeah, she might be in danger, but the look on his face right as he left was one of irritation, not really fear. Could he easily kill somebody out of irritation? Or was the bad boy who'd just left her arms joking? She wasn't sure if that was the case—or if he had every intention of killing whoever had penetrated his home fortress.

She didn't know this man, what he was capable of doing. Just because he fought for the country didn't mean he wasn't just another bad boy, hell-bent on getting what he wanted no matter the cost. Or worse, willing to kill someone for no real reason.

One thing was for sure–she wasn't going to sit around, waiting to learn just what kind of man he was. Oh, no.

She was going to find out, starting now.

CHAPTER NINE

"WHAT THE HELL, MAN?" Hunter barked when he yanked open the door. "You set off my alarm."

Gauge smiled at him, but the prick didn't look the least bit apologetic. "Wanted to test your security system."

"Bullshit. You're lucky I don't pop a cap in your ass right now."

"Dude," Gauge said, taking a wide berth around Hunter as he stepped in. "You need to chill."

"At least I didn't have to witness a coldblooded murder," Maya said from behind him, and he whirled.

"Jesus, woman. I asked you to stay back. He could've been someone breakin' in to hurt you."

Maya smiled, but the look didn't give him any warm fuzzies. He knew a pissed off woman when he saw one. What had he done? He couldn't help they got interrupted. He should punch Gauge in the balls just for that alone. And he probably would when he got over being irate about dude breaching his security. The second the sensor on his wristband tripped, he'd gone into full alert mode, but the bypass code flashing back at him was the one he'd given his teammates in case they ever needed access to his property. He knew it was one of the guys. He just hadn't been sure which one or why the access code hadn't been entered at the first checkpoint. If it had, the alarm wouldn't have sounded even if it had been tripped.

It also didn't explain why one of them was here in the middle of the day.

"Obviously, he's not." She crossed her arms and took a big breath. "I'm going to take a shower. I feel dirty."

He narrowed his eyes and opened his mouth to ask her if she was talking about what happened between them, but either way he could see her blaming him. If she really *was* dirty, it was still his fault for tackling her to the ground outside. But if she meant it as an innuendo, he didn't want to address any of that in front of Gauge. He figured it'd be best to ignore whatever meaning was lurking behind her words. "Be careful with your leg. There's medicine under the sink."

She harrumphed and turned, stomping out as if she was a mad baby chick. He had to fight the smile that threatened to form. Oh yeah, her feathers were ruffled.

"So...how's it going?" Gauge asked slowly, not even attempting to hide the smile in his voice.

Hunter cocked his head to the side as he turned. He had no intention of discussing anything personal relating to Maya with any of his teammates. As far as he was concerned, *that* had nothing to do with them. "Just peachy, brother. You gonna tell me what the hell you're doing here, setting off my shit? You know it doesn't need testing." He narrowed his gaze at him before pushing the door closed without looking and walking to the couch.

Gauge chuckled as he followed and sat on the other end. He rubbed his hands together slowly before clasping them between his legs. "Nah, dude. I know your system is top-notch, but you've never harbored someone here before. I wanted to check a few things out."

Hunter leaned back, crossing his arms. "Did I pass muster?"

"Yeah, it's good. Oh, c'mon, don't glare at me like that. You know your property borders the Wildlife Management area on the east. Anybody—"

"No-fucking-body can cross my property line anywhere without me knowing."

"Famous last words, but hey," Gauge added, lifting his hands. "You're doing your job. I'm doing mine."

Hunter stiffened. "Meaning?"

"Knock that chip off your shoulder, Hunter. You know what I'm talkin' about."

Yes, he did, but that didn't mean he had to like it. "So Bear has you watching me?"

"I'm backing you up. Nothing wrong with that."

"I thought we were swamped at the garage," Hunter said as he forced himself to relax and not take the invasion personally.

"He pushed back a few of the scheduled gigs and Roc is flying through that '55 restore. We're good."

Bear was rescheduling their jobs? The man never did that. Not even when Colonel was still around. To Bear, once something was on the calendar, that shit was engraved in granite.

Something prickled as he watched Gauge rub his hands together again. "What's going on?" There was something Gauge wasn't telling him.

His colleague's breath whooshed out as he faced him. "Oberman has mafia connections."

Hunter stilled, faking calm indifference while his

insides roared. "We knew that was a possibility based on the attorney who bailed him out." He knew that guy was bad news and the threat of illegal ties was great. Having it confirmed, though, hit too close to home. Yes, Hunter had dealt with many crime families and their affiliates while working with the Bang Shift, but it was never easy. He always had to push aside his past to confront the evil of the present.

"Yeah, man, we did, but we found that connection is with Alonzo Rudolph."

Hunter saw red. That was a name he hadn't heard aloud in years. A name that was only safe to utter in dreams. Rudolph had tried ruining Hunter's life by pulling him into his drug-trafficking crime family when he'd been young and naive. Thankfully, he'd gotten out before he officially got in, but that didn't change the fact that he had and would continue to hide from that man for the rest of his life.

No one knew of Hunter's past, and he wanted to keep it that way. But that didn't mean he wouldn't know of the various organized crime groups in the world. They were hired too often to play dumb on that.

"What does some lieutenant in a Columbian gang have to do with Oberman?"

Gauge flashed a smile at him, and for some reason, nerves settled in the pit of his stomach. "Alonzo Rudolph has moved up quickly within the family biz. He's now the underboss. Not bad for a man who started out as a soldier and moved quickly into a post where one of his duties was to recruit enforcers. But then, you know all about that, don't you?"

Gauge shifted in his seat, not breaking eye contact. Hunter was a statue, unable to move, unwilling to give anything away. But his heart was racing, blood rushing in his ears, vision hazy as he tried frantically to assess just how much Gauge knew.

Hunter refused to flinch, knowing the man across from him was watching his every move and analyzing everything.

"Yes," he said slowly. "I knew about Rudolph's past, but his recent promotion is news to me."

Gauge's jaw ticked, obviously not pleased with the vague response.

Hunter stared back him.

Neither said another word for what felt like hours, but was probably only seconds.

Gauge was like a brother to him. The other guys had been slower to accept him into the group, but Hunter had been long past the "newbie" crap. The man had proven himself worthy of his post and did a damn good job...at least on the contract side of things. He still had some stuff to learn about cars...but right now it was painfully clear just how well his colleague excelled with his stealthier duties.

Hunter refused to show his hand first, though. He'd learned a long time ago never give up more than was necessary.

The two were at a stalemate.

After several more hours-long seconds, Gauge took a deep breath and said on the exhale, "Do you honestly believe the FBI would work with anyone they haven't fully investigated?"

Shit. Gauge knew. He fucking knew about Hunter's past. Didn't matter just how much the man had found out because it was obviously enough. He should have known the feds would've dug into his history. Hell, he'd seen them do that a hundred times with other people.

And Gauge was an agent. He'd worked undercover for the feds for years without the team knowing it. It wasn't until Xan came to town that his cover was blown. If any of them understood the inner workings of the government, it was Gauge.

Then an even bleaker thought came to him.

"Who all knows?" There was no use acting as if he didn't understand what Gauge meant. They were beyond that now. Besides, he needed to know the numbers. What he was dealing with.

"Everyone."

"Goddammit." Hunter jumped from the couch and started pacing. "It was a long time ago. I screwed up, and I fixed it." He had. He'd royally effed up, and no matter how hard he tried, he'd never be able to make it better. Not completely. Didn't mean he couldn't make the effort, which he did. Every day.

"You're making me dizzy. Talk to me, man."

He stopped by the wall opposite Gauge and turned to face him. "We all make mistakes when we're young. Rudolph was mine. I got a fake I.D. before I headed to Texas. No one knew the real me there. Maybe I'd figured out my dumb ass was making a mistake seeking out the quick money, and I wanted to be sure it'd be easy for me to run back home. I don't know, but I thank God everyday I had the brains to lie about my identity back then."

"You still think he's coming after you one day."

It wasn't a question.

Hunter shrugged. "He's not known for his leniency. And the man's pride is the size of Texas. I'm willing to bet there aren't too many men left breathing who turned him down on anything."

"Good point." Gauge smiled as he shook his head slightly.

Hunter frowned. "What?"

"I've known for years, dude. So has Bear. Colonel told him, which meant he was also privy to the info, not that what the traitor knew has anything to do with us now." He shrugged. "I mean, that man was very methodical about why he'd brought everyone together. He'd probably had the intention of using your connection one day. Who knows?"

"Yeah." Hunter hadn't thought about it like that. There'd probably be all kinds of revelations come to light about whatever the Colonel's ultimate plan was that only time and lots of investigation could provide.

"But *I* knew because I was briefed on everybody before taking the job out here."

"And the others?"

"Monday," Gauge said on a sigh. "We had a meeting after you bolted from the garage to discuss what Bear and I learned while meeting with our federal contacts."

"And nobody cared to tell me?" Hunter narrowed his gaze.

"Dude. You left." Gauge chuckled. When Hunter didn't find the humor in that, he added, "Lighten up. We all have a job to do. Like I said, the news of your old connection to Rudolph was brought up, but it wasn't negative. Hell, the feds, Bear, and me already knew. The issue at hand was your safety *now*, not your past."

"Mine?" Hunter said, moving toward the couch. He still couldn't wrap his head around the fact that everybody knew about his past, but he didn't have time to come to terms with that at this moment.

No, right now, he needed to get back into work mode, because apparently, he was out of the loop on some pretty important things. He wanted brought up to speed immediately so he could figure shit out.

"Yes, the consensus is that this looks a little too coincidental."

"What does that mean?" Hunter mumbled a curse as he tried to rein in renewed irritation. "Jesus, man, spit it out."

"That Jake Oberman 'the Doberman' is an enforcer for Rudolph who just happened to be involved with your sister's roommate."

White-hot anger surged through him, but he forced himself to remain calm. "My sister? So you think I've been made? That they're going to get to me through my sister?" How he managed to get the words out without roaring, he didn't know.

"Sorry, man, but it's looking like that." When Hunter surged to his feet, Gauge was right there with him, in his face, finger shoved into his chest. "Cool it."

Hunter pushed the other man off him. "No. My sister's in danger, no one told me, and you want me to calm down? *Fuck* you." He was already calculating how long it'd take to get to her campus if he drove ninety most of the way. Not soon enough.

Jesus, so not soon enough.

Gauge grabbed his arm, forcing him to stop and look at him. "I need you to detach."

He laughed mirthlessly before training the coldest gaze he could muster on his colleague. "No way."

"I know she's your sister—"

"The only family I have left," he said, cutting off Gauge.

"I get that. I do. But she has both an FBI agent and Blade watching her six. She's not alone. Ever." Gauge stepped closer and dropped his voice. "What if this is a trap for you, huh? What if you go stomping down there to get her and walk right into a set up?"

Hunter scoffed at that. "I know how to protect myself."

"I know you do. But you can't defend yourself against a sniper."

"Neither can Heather," he roared, the thread of his control snapping.

Gauge grabbed both of Hunter's shoulders. "Yeah, okay, bad example. But I hate to break it to you, if Heather was the intended target, she'd already be dead. Think, man. This isn't *about* her. Hell, all we know for sure is that Jake was dating her roommate, so it might not have anything to do with you either. That's worst case scenario out of a lot of fucking possibilities. We need to get to the bottom of things and keep our damn heads screwed on, ya feel me?"

The breath that Hunter took was ragged, so he forced more air into his burning lungs. He knew Gauge was right, but that didn't mean he had to like it. At all. After several seconds of getting his temper under control, and not doing a great job of it, he asked, "And how do we do that?"

Gauge patted Hunter's shoulder before dropping his hands. "It's time we talked to Maya again. We need to know everything she knows about Jake."

With anger clouding him, he'd forgotten about her storming off earlier. She'd been mad about something. What, he didn't know.

And he was almost as worried about finding out the reason for her reaction as he was discovering everything she knew.

Almost.

————

THE SHOWER HAD REDDENED Maya's skin, but it was a good kind of burn. The heat of the water helped distract her for as long as she could stand it, which had been until the temperature began to drop. Then it wasn't warm enough to be effective against thoughts of Hunter, and no way was she taking a cold shower.

Didn't matter if she'd needed that earlier. Her raging hormones were back to a manageable simmer—not as low as she'd wished, but beggars couldn't be choosers. She would take whatever reprieve she could get from the growing attraction until she could squash it altogether. Because she would. There was no other choice.

Had she not learned her lesson before? She would laugh at her reflection if she didn't think it would turn into a pathetic crying fit. Why was she drawn to bad boys? Was it because she'd been so sheltered growing up? It wasn't as if she hadn't ever had a boyfriend before.

Nice boyfriends. Ones she'd met at church or her small private school.

Maybe the bad-boy appeal was something every girl fought. *I mean they write books and movies about tough dudes.* Surely it was something ingrained within the female population. Otherwise, Hollywood wouldn't bother. Maybe it was something strong women were able to resist—or at least learned to resist.

A life lesson Maya totally missed. It wouldn't be that big of a stretch considering her conservative upbringing. But it was hard for her to justify her shortcomings right at this moment.

And it's not a freakin' shortcoming.

She couldn't help it she didn't know how to deal with men like Hunter. Like Jake.

Okay, maybe it wasn't fair to put them in the same category, but it wasn't as if she was working with a complete knowledge base here. She pushed away any thoughts of inexperience *and* guilt and got dressed. She succeeded in keeping her mind off all things Hunter while she donned fresh clothes and brushed her still-wet hair. If any thoughts of their impromptu make-out session started surfacing, she hummed or paid extra attention to her pores to help refocus. She couldn't go back down that road yet. It would have to wait until she knew she could be alone longer than thirty minutes without the threat of seeing the object of her frustration again.

After draping her towel over the shower curtain, she opened the door...and stilled. Hunter stood at the end of the hall, arms crossed, watching the bathroom door.

"Gauge and I need to talk to you."

Okay, *twenty* minutes, not thirty. She'd been too generous before.

"Fine." She pushed back her shoulders and walked toward him, facing ahead. No way in hell was she going to look at him if she didn't have to. As she began to pass him, though, he reached out and wrapped his hand around her elbow, stopping her. She leaned in, his breath working through her wet stands.

"Don't know why you're mad. We'll talk about *that* later." He dropped his voice so much she had a hard time making out the rest of what he said. "That's between us." Yeah, she had a hard time hearing him, but she got the gist. Hunter didn't want her telling Gauge about what had happened between them. She wouldn't do that, but why did he feel the need to make sure? Was he embarrassed? Did it not mean anything to him?

Hurt and humiliation soared, battling for dominance. She reared back to fire off something at him, but the moment their gazes met, he grabbed her, pulling her closer to him.

"Don't. Whatever you're thinking. Don't."

Stunned by the fierceness of his words, all she could do was nod slowly.

He gentled his hold and leaned even closer. Jeez, any closer and he'd be touching her all over. He opened his mouth and her pulse raced. Was he going to say something or kiss her?

"Dude. I can see your backside. Whatever you're doing can wait 'til later."

Hunter cursed as he pulled away from her.

"Like after I'm long gone," Gauge muttered.

"I got it," Hunter said over his shoulder. Then he looked at her. "Let's go."

He guided her to the couch and nudged her down before sitting on the other side of her. She didn't look at him, though. She stared at the other man sitting in the chair across from them.

"Hello again." He smiled.

"Hi," she squeaked. She cleared her throat and said it clearer the second time before adding, "Hunter said you needed to talk to me."

"Yeah." He leaned forward, clasping his hands together between his legs. "We have some questions about your ex-boyfriend."

Maya sighed, shutting her eyes and nodding. When she opened them again, the pleasant smile that had graced Gauge's face was gone. She couldn't put her finger on the look he was now sporting, but it couldn't be good. She bit her lip, waiting.

"How did you meet him?"

She shrugged. "He's a student at—"

"No," Gauge said, cutting her off. "He's not."

She blinked, trying to understand what the man said. Shaking her head, she said, "Yes, he goes to—"

"No—"

"Gauge," Hunter snapped. "Knock it off. This isn't an interrogation." He looked at Maya. "What he means is how and where you met Jake. Specifically," he said, his tone much gentler than the other guy.

"I, er, I mean, I saw him around campus. He flirted with me at the coffee shop a few times. I didn't know how to take it at first. I wasn't used to guys being so forward with me." She looked down and played with her hands. "I was partying at the bar with Heather one night when he asked me out the first time." She shrugged. "I said no, but he persisted. We started going out a few weeks after that."

"So you never had any classes with him?" Hunter asked. She looked at him and frowned. It felt a little weird talking about her ex to a guy she'd just—*not going there*.

"No. He's older than me and a business major. No way would I study that, and he's already taken his core classes. There's no reason why we'd ever be in the same classes."

"Do you have any friends in common?" Gauge asked.

Her gaze cut to him. "No." His question hadn't been as forceful, but she wasn't sure where this was going.

"Ever been to his house?"

Heat flooded her cheeks. "No," she muttered. God, why did she have to feel embarrassed about that? She was a grown woman. There wasn't anything wrong with her being at her boyfriend's place. If she ever had been. "He, um, always came to the dorm."

"What do you mean by that?" Gauge asked.

Yep, her face was on fire now. Why couldn't a hole form and swallow her? Make her disappear from this conversation? She could slink back into the couch and keep praying for a miracle void to engulf her, or she could confront this guy. Okay, maybe she wasn't that ballsy, but she could pretend.

"He was my boyfriend," she said in a shaky voice. "What do you think I mean?" She raised her eyebrows, challenging him, and he smirked.

"I don't need to know how good of a fuck he was."

Hunter stiffened and she gasped at Gauge's crudeness, but it didn't take long for her to find her voice. "Good, because I don't kiss and tell. You have something you seriously need to know, then ask. Otherwise, you can go screw yourself."

Gauge held up his hands. "My apologies. That was out of line." *No kidding*, she thought. He took a deep breath as he leaned in. "But we've learned some disturbing things about Mr. Jake, so we need to know more about why he was in your life."

"Like what?" she asked, narrowing her gaze.

Gauge's gaze shot to Hunter. Maya glanced at him, too, when the other man didn't look at her. Hunter sat still as a statue until finally the slightest nod came from him. It was as if Gauge was asking for his permission. Why would he do that? The jerk hadn't seemed to care about anyone's feelings a few seconds ago.

Or maybe it was just hers he didn't care about. She didn't understand why that bothered her, but it did. Her palms got slick as she waited for Gauge to continue.

"Jake Oberman is in the mafia."

She blinked.

Her mouth opened.

She swallowed.

She stared.

When neither of the guys said anything else, she burst out laughing. Like, tears in her eyes, full on fits. She could barely breathe. This was this most ridiculous thing she'd ever heard. When she finally could manage words, she asked, "What?" But still giggled. Totally absurd. "That's insane."

"It's not a laughing matter, Maya," Gauge said.

"He's being serious," Hunter added.

Her humor died an instant death, and she immediately felt the blood drain from her face. "What?" she asked again, this time barely a whisper. Were they for real?

"Your ex is an enforcer in a crime family we, uh...keep track of."

Her mind raced. They had to be mistaken. Jake wasn't a criminal. Okay, she figured he was capable of vandalizing her car, but what they were talking about was so far beyond that it wasn't in the same hemisphere. No way were they right about this... Were they?

But... What if there was some truth to this news? Why else would they say it? And what did it all mean? She couldn't keep up with her flying thoughts, but what she blurted out wasn't anything she'd consciously considered, a whole new reality slamming her in the face.

"Because SEALs do that, right? Keep track of the mafia?" she asked incredulously. Maybe she'd meant to throw the attention off herself, but when he broke eye contact, she felt the truth settle into her bones. "You're not in the military."

"No," was all he said before looking at Gauge. "I don't think she knows anything."

"She could be a good actor." Gauge shrugged.

"Wait, what?" she said, glancing back and forth between them. "You think I knew about this? I'm not even sure I *believe* this." She glared at Hunter. "And *I'm* not the one holding out in the information department, Hunter."

An image of the letter Jake had left in her car flashed in her mind, but she ignored it. That letter didn't matter. Not anymore.

"You're on a need-to-know basis," Gauge said.

"I wasn't talking to you," she yelled before getting to her feet. She stared at Hunter, who looked too calm, too unrepentant. "You want to know about me and Jake? Fine. I thought he was a student with a bad-boy streak who lived in an apartment off campus. He excited me, but I later realized his behavior was sadistic, bordering on abusive. But hell, what do I know? When I realized what I'd gotten into, I. Cut. It. Off. But, guess what? He's not the type to take no for an answer, so he stalked me. Followed me around. Made it blatantly obvious sometimes, but even when I didn't see him, I still had the sensation I was being watched. I don't know where he lives. I don't know what he does for a living. I obviously didn't handle the situation well at all. He saw an easy target, and I fell for his lies. Sheltered little Maya got duped by the illusive bad boy. That what you want to hear? Because it seems to me you know more about him than I ever did."

She turned and left the room. If either of them came after her, she would blow up. Again. She was steaming mad.

And confused as hell.

Jake was in the mob? Was it true? If so, how could she have missed that? He could've been so much more dangerous than she'd ever realized, and she'd been too naive to see the signs.

Or ask him any serious questions.

She'd let his sexy charm woo her stupid.

Just like she'd done with Hunter.

And that reminded her of even more crap she'd just

learned. Hunter wasn't even in the military. Really? He'd lied to her

But what also hurt was knowing he wasn't the only one who'd lied. So had her best friend.

Somewhere deep inside, she knew there was probably a good explanation for Heather's betrayal, like her friend probably felt it wasn't her place to talk about her brother's secrets, but Maya didn't want to be logical right now.

It was apparent she couldn't be trusted with logic anyhow. Even after she'd told herself she was through with bad boys, here she was, letting another one cloud her judgment. But it wasn't even the men's fault. It was hers. This wasn't the idyllic fifties they were living in. She should know better than to take anyone at face value. *Should.* She obviously didn't. Yeah, logic totally evaded her.

She would learn, though. She'd been dealt two big lessons already. She'd made her mistakes in the romance department, challenged love and lost. Not anymore.

She wasn't foolish enough to believe it was safe for her to go back to school just yet, especially after discovering Jake's real job, but that didn't mean she couldn't do better at fighting the temptation Hunter presented. She'd done a crappy job so far and would probably have more difficulty sticking to her guns. But if she got weak, all she'd have to do was remind herself he'd lied to her, too.

And no matter how sexy a man was, she couldn't be with anyone she didn't trust.

CHAPTER TEN

HUNTER TOSSED the wrench out from under the car he'd been working on as he cursed. He'd started working on his old man's piece of shit car again this past week as an excuse to stay out of the house. The junked-up Chevelle had seen better days, even after he and his dad started the restoration. After his dad died, though, Hunter couldn't bring himself to continue it. Not for a few years anyway, and then it was only for a couple of hours here and there. It wasn't until this week that he'd thrown himself into it again.

He didn't care if he was using the car as his reason to avoid the woman only yards away. He should thank her for freeing up the space in his garage when he was done.

"And you're a dick," he muttered, knowing he'd never be that mean. Not to her. Jesus, he didn't know what to think of her or why she ignited things within him. But she did. For that reason alone, he couldn't say something hateful like that.

"Hey now, most people think I'm pretty awesome," Brody said.

Hunter rolled from under the car, smile already on his

face. "What are you doing here?" He wasn't complaining. He welcomed the new distraction.

Brody leaned against the built-in tool cabinet and crossed his arms. He shook his head as a slight humorless laugh slipped out. "Xan figured you'd need a break from your ward."

Hunter reached out and grabbed a rag before hoisting himself up. He wiped his hands as he smiled at Brody. "Thank her for me, would ya?"

"Yeah," he said slowly. "You can thank her yourself. She's in your house."

Hunter's smile slipped. Why was Xan here? "Oh."

"With Roxie."

"Er, why?" He tossed the rag to the side and propped his hands on his hips.

"Sorry, man." He shrugged. "Your houseguest lives in the Dallas-Forth Worth area. Much larger than Little Rock. She wants to talk shopping. For the wedding." He sighed and rubbed the bridge of his nose. "This is gonna cost me a fuck ton of money."

Hunter couldn't feel his fingers. He fisted his hands, released. Nope, still couldn't feel them. His heart pounded, ears rang. What the hell was wrong with him? He liked Xan, and he'd grown up with Roxie. It shouldn't matter if they were alone with Maya. He trusted them. And if Xan wanted to talk about her wedding with Maya—

Blood rushed to his head. *Oh fuck me.* It was *Maya* and *wedding* mingling in his brain that caused the reaction. Hell, no. No. He wasn't the marrying kind. He couldn't ever risk that with anyone. Besides, he didn't know Maya that well. They hadn't even had sex. Why would she elicit that kind of reaction from him when chicks he'd banged casually for years never had?

He slammed the door shut on that thought. It didn't matter.

When he looked at Brody again, the man continued to wallow in the financial woes of planning a wedding. Rather than think of Maya, Hunter would focus on his sister. He could relate to Brody on that level. At least Xan didn't think plastic should be a precious metal.

"I feel ya," he finally said. "Heather gets an idea in her head and she wants the best. Doesn't matter how much it'll cost."

Brody's hand fell to his side as he chuckled. "Dude, I would never say this to Xan, but the wedding is bringing out the fashion diva from her past life."

Hunter whistled low.

"Yeah. Nothing is good enough. The venues we've looked at are too *commercial* looking. The dresses are too traditional. Nothing is right. These are her words, of course. I'd get married on a pig farm today if she'd let me."

"Bridezilla."

"Bride what?" Brody reared back.

"Bridezilla. It's what happens when a normally sweet girl turns into a raging monster during her wedding planning and such."

Brody's face turned dark. "And how the hell do you know that?"

Uh-oh. Hunter wasn't insulting Xan. "It's a thing." He lifted his hands and took a tentative step backward. "There's even a T.V. show about it. Heather watched it all the damn time."

Brody looked down, frowning. "So it's gonna get worse?" he groaned.

Hunter relaxed. "Sorry, man, but yeah. I don't know why they do that. It's a woman thing, I guess."

Brody walked over to the Chevelle and poked around under the hood. "I don't know what to do. Everything I suggest, she shuts down."

Seeing Brody look somewhat vulnerable eased a little of the tension that had been building for days. Hunter walked to the car and leaned over it, facing his friend from the other side. Never in his life had he imagined he'd be talking wedding planning in his garage while tinkering with a car.

But this was what Brody needed.

And Hunter knew he could benefit from the different topic.

"What have you suggested?"

Brody looked up, shocked. "Huh?"

"C'mon, man. About the wedding. What have you suggested?"

He blew out a breath. "Everything from renting a ball room downtown to getting married in a little country church."

Hunter nodded slowly. "And why didn't she like those ideas?"

"Um," he hesitated, looking up. "Ball room was too fancy. Convention center was too sterile. Country church was too dated."

"Too dated?" Hunter frowned.

Brody stood and rested his arm across the open hood. "Yeah, it had paneling. I mentioned it because she said she wanted a country chic wedding."

"What's that?"

"Fuck, I don't know." Brody shoved away from the car and began to walk back and forth alongside it. "The best I can tell is that it's a classy wedding with a country feel."

"Classy and country. Those words don't go together."

"I know," Brody muttered. "I'd prefer it to be as private

as possible. For security reasons, you know? But damn, it's like she's going for something very specific, but she doesn't know what that is. It's like she's being difficult on purpose."

"Bridezilla," Hunter said matter-of-factly.

Brody barked out a laugh, and Hunter joined in. When they both finally caught their breath, Brody said, "Thanks, man. I needed that."

"Anytime."

After picking up a socket wrench, Brody leaned over the car again as he twirled it. "Seriously, though, if you think of a place that might even sorta fit the country chic she wants, for the love of God, let me know."

Hunter chuckled. "I will...hmm." An idea came to him. It was so far out there, he almost laughed. It was almost ridiculous he'd even thought it. It had disaster written on it on so many levels, but—

"What? If you have an idea, you better spit it out."

He nodded slowly. "Yeah. Um, Roc has that huge barn on his property he's almost finished building. Don't know why he even bothered with it since he doesn't like horses. Says they need too much attention. But it's new and clean. And private." He shrugged.

"Roc?"

"Hey, you *know* how I feel about him." Hunter wasn't surprised he'd zeroed in on the mention of their colleague and not the fact that he'd suggested they get married in a *barn*.

Brody immediately started shaking his head. "He'd never go for it. He's too selfish to do anything for anybody else."

"If your lovely fiancée is in full monster-mode, maybe he won't be able to turn her down."

"Yeah, but a barn?" Brody frowned. "I wasn't joking

when I said I'd get married on a farm. I even mentioned it to her and she got so mad I thought she was going to make me sleep on the couch."

Hunter stepped closer to him. "Okay, but a farm has a bunch of stinky animals and cow patties everywhere. Not surprised she doesn't want to smell shit as she takes her vows. Think about it...Roc's barn is animal free still. Hell, he doesn't even have a dog. Plus, he's building that thing from reclaimed barn wood, so it'd look authentic. It's about as rustic chic as you can get."

Brody was silent for a while as he tapped his chin slowly. Finally, he said, "*Country* chic, but you make some good points. Wouldn't hurt to mention it to Xan."

"True."

Brody pointed at him. "But if she doesn't like it, I'm blaming you."

"Throw me under the bus, dude. I don't care." He smiled.

Brody picked up a rag and started rubbing a spot on the frame, but it didn't seem to Hunter that the man was really too focused on the car. "Rusted."

Hunter took a closer look. "Not all the way through."

Without moving his head, Brody glanced up. "Miss you at the shop." He looked down and continued to rub, confirming his theory the man's mind was somewhere else. "Be glad when this case is over."

Hunter swallowed, remembering the conversation he'd had with Gauge. Everybody at the shop knew about his past. It wasn't something he was proud of, and facing it with the guys he worked with was going to be hard. It was better to start addressing it now. "Look, about Rudolph—"

"Been looking into him," Brody said without taking his focus away from his mindless task. "He's coming up clean. Hasn't even stepped foot in the States in almost a year."

After letting that information sink in, Hunter said, "I mean about my past—"

Brody stood and looked at him. "Don't, brother. We all have pasts. I'm exhibit A though Z. Living in the past screws up your present. And your future."

"Not all of us are lucky enough to have our memories taken," Hunter said casually, not trying to be offensive. Brody had worked for another mafia family, true, but he didn't have to live with flashbacks to his darker time. His friend's amnesia was, in many ways, a blessing.

"I'm grateful for a lot of things." He pointed toward the open overhead door. "That woman over there? She's my life now. That's all that matters. What I did...what *any* of us did before we woke up today? Yeah, none of that's important. You feel me?"

Hunter nodded, but Brody had been really lucky. The stars had aligned. The angels had sung, and the heavens had smiled down on him. That didn't happen often. Hunter was happy for the man. Truly. Xan was a special kind of woman, though.

"I know she is."

Hunter's gaze flew to Brody as he realized he'd spoken that last part out loud.

"But that doesn't mean she's the only special lady out there."

He smiled at Brody, but that was the only response he could muster, because he knew the truth. There were other special ladies out there. Of course there were.

But Hunter wouldn't let one in his heart. Maya had gotten too close already, and he had to keep her from finding the tiniest of cracks in his armor. If she did, he would be powerless when it came to her. He couldn't allow that.

Brody clapped Hunter on the shoulder. "C'mon. Let's check on the women and grab a bite to eat. All this talk about weddings and shit is making me hungry."

Hunter followed along, a smile on his face, while he reinforced the steel around his heart.

———

MAYA BLINKED at the glass of iced tea in her hands, remembering the two women who'd been sitting on the couch earlier today. She also remembered the man they'd come with. He'd been one of the guys at the garage. One of the *biggest* guys. Hunter was big, but that guy had been huge. So when he'd brought those ladies into the house and said they were here to keep her company, she hadn't argued. They'd spent the better part of the afternoon chatting about Xan's wedding to the big bruiser, Brody. *Better her than me.* The man had terrified her.

But when the guys had come back in from Hunter's shop, she'd envied Xan. Brody had given her his undivided attention, doing even the smallest things for her without seeming to think first. It had come naturally to him to take her glass from her when she'd finished drinking, stand when she did, help her around the coffee table when she needed to pee. It'd been sweet, but it was more than that. Brody was a man in tune with his woman. Maya had never seen anything like that before. A couple of times, she stole glances at Hunter when Brody was doing something for Xan.

He'd been watching them too, with a furrow between

his eyebrows. She'd wondered what he was thinking, and then cursed herself for going there.

Once, he caught her staring at him. Rather than look away, she'd been trapped by his gaze. Hunter had been the one to break the spell, but even then it took several seconds before he glanced away. It seemed hard for him to do, tear his gaze away, but she'd quickly attributed that to wishful thinking.

Then she'd berated herself for even thinking that. It didn't matter what he thought or how difficult things were for him. She needed to stick to her guns.

Oh yeah? Then why are you taking the man a drink?

She sighed as she put the glass on the counter, losing her nerve. Her intention wasn't anything more than calling a truce. Hunter had avoided her all week, staying out in his garage. Even with Brody, Xan, and Roxie around, he'd gone out of his way to avoid her. The five of them had gone into town to eat lunch at Stoby's, a little restaurant known for its cheese dip they'd all bragged about. Maya had been jumping at the chance to leave the house, and had been surprised Hunter was allowing it. Any excitement she'd felt vanished after they arrived. Why? Hunter. He'd whispered something to Roxie as they walked in, and Roxie had immediately taken Maya by the arm, pulling her to a booth in the front. She'd been nudged into it and Roxie had slid in beside her. Brody and Xan had taken the bench opposite them with Hunter pulling up a chair from a neighboring table. Maya knew what he'd done. He'd asked Roxie to sit beside her so *he* wouldn't have to. It shouldn't have mattered.

It had.

The fact that he'd been going out of his way to stay away from her was bordering on the ridiculous. She was tired of it. Maybe it had helped her keep her resolve in the beginning, but now it sort of pissed her off. She was stuck here, and he wasn't doing anything to make her entrapment better.

But she knew attacking him with the truth wouldn't do any good. She needed to be nice. Feeling a little more confident, she picked up the glass of tea again. This time, she didn't hesitate. She walked out of the kitchen and onto the porch where she'd spied him sitting.

He'd been sharpening a knife or something and looked up as she opened the door. She kept her gaze on him as she shut it behind her. God, why did he have to look so sexy? Sweat glistened his brow, hair stuck to his forehead in a few places, eyes were bright even in the night, strong jaw flexing as his stare bored into her.

Stop it. This obsession on his crazy good looks had to stop. She licked her lips as she moved toward him.

"Brought you a drink."

His eyes grew slightly wider before he offered an appreciative smile and reached for the glass. "Thanks." He took a big gulp and she averted her gaze. She would not look at his long, thick neck.

"So," she started slowly, looking out into the dark yard. "Been sharpening knives?"

Good lord. She sounded like a dork.

"Not exactly."

The sheepish way he said that drew her attention back to him. She knew he'd been holding a knife. She couldn't have missed the glint of the blade earlier even if she'd tried to avoid seeing it. But when she saw the stick he held up with fresh wood exposed, she realized she'd jumped to the wrong conclusion. Was he carving something? Did regular people do that sort of thing?

"Whittling."

So he was trying to create something out of that wood. She could go along with that or try to be funny to lighten the mood even more. It wouldn't hurt to try.

"Ah, you're making a stake. I'd heard there was a big vampire problem out here."

He laughed, eyes dancing as he looked at her. "Major vamp problem."

Feeling a little more at ease, she walked toward where he sat on the steps. His smile faltered when she reached him, so she continued her stride past him as if that had been her intention all along ."You're joking, but Heather *told* me how big the mosquitoes get out here," she said as she reached the grass.

"Bloodthirsty little fuckers," he said with a wink.

She ignored what that little flirtatious gesture did to her hormones. It had come so effortlessly from him, she'd do her best not to think anything of it.

That was easier said than done.

Taking a couple of steps backward so she could watch him as she talked, she said, "Stakes could come in handy—*ow*. What the...?"

She jumped to the side, grabbing her ankle. Had she stepped on something? Kicked a branch or something? It looked like some kind of stick.

"Wh—oh fuck." Hunter was there in an instant. She would've gasped at how quickly he'd moved if her mind wasn't reeling at what she thought she'd just seen.

He lifted her into his arms and leapt onto the porch, away from the grassy area she'd just been. It happened so fast she almost missed the rustling on the ground as something moved.

"Is that—"

"Did it get you?"

Her ankle screamed as she reached for it. Even more confirmation that she hadn't been seeing things. "Oh my god, I got bit by a snake?" she screeched.

"Copperhead," he muttered as he shoved his way into the house. He jostled her in his grip as he dug in his pocket for something. "We gotta get you to the hospital."

Her gaze snapped from her throbbing leg to him. "Why? Is it poisonous?" A snake was a snake was a snake. How could he tell just by looking at it what kind it was or if it was even poisonous?

The grim look he gave her was all the answer she needed. He cursed and hit something on his phone. "Taking her to the hospital. She tangoed with a Copperhead. Yeah. Need you to get ahold of the doc. Have the anti-venom ready. Later."

He ended the call, shoved the phone back into his pocket, and grabbed his wallet. Within two strides, he was back at the front door.

"Wait. I need my shoes."

"No."

He reached back to slam the door and then moved toward the steps.

"But the snake," she protested.

"It'll be gone now. If not, it'll be dead," he muttered.

"What?" She looked frantically at the grass as he walked toward his truck. There could be more of them out there waiting to attack her.

Before she could say anything else, he'd deposited her onto the passenger' seat. "Seatbelt," he barked, and shut the door. He was in the driver's seat making gravel spew before she could order her hands to follow his instructions.

She grabbed the side of the door to steady herself as he

hit the main road. He was driving like a crazy person, his eyes almost cold as he glared at everything in their path.

"We'll be there in less than ten. You'll be fine." He still didn't look at her.

She opened her mouth to respond, but the only sound that came out was a scream as the pain in her ankle turned into a raging fire.

Hunter's head whipped to the side and he grabbed her hand. Momentarily shocked out of her agonizing pain, she looked at their joined hands—loving the feel of him touching her again—then at him, his gaze now softened as he watched her.

"It'll be okay, baby," he whispered.

There was no mistaking this endearment for general southern charm. It was meant just for her.

It made her heart soar, just as her world went black.

CHAPTER ELEVEN

"Maya? Maya, baby, stay with me. *Fuck.*" She was out. The pain was too intense for her. Hell, he knew what it was like getting bitten. He'd had his own run-in with a snake growing up. It had been a baby, not that it'd mattered. The venom had been just as potent as if it had been an adult. He'd cried all the way to the hospital while his mom chewed his dad a new asshole for taking his eyes off him long enough for Hunter to get hurt. At the time, he'd felt it hadn't been fair of his mom to act like that, but now? Shit, he understood why she had. She'd been terrified.

He hated feeling like this. So fucking helpless.

Snakes were a part of life out here, but that didn't make them any more welcome. Especially the poisonous ones. Thankfully, he knew how to tell snakes and any other dangerous creepy-crawlies apart from the non-threatening ones. God, he should've been paying attention to her. He knew snakes were on his land. He had the forestry land to the other side of him and both the lake and river were not far. Maybe if he hadn't been so focused on how hot her ass was in those pants, she wouldn't be in this situation now.

When his phone went off, he reluctantly let go of her hand to answer it.

"Doc's headed to E.R. What's your E.T.A.?" Bear asked.

Hunter looked at the clock and glanced at the road. "Six minutes."

"Ask for Sawyer when you get there. We don't want any record of her being seen."

"Got it."

"How is she?" Bear asked after a long pause.

"Chatting the Sandman." And driving him fucking crazy. Still.

"Good. If she's out cold then she's not panicking, which means her heart isn't racing, pumping that venom through her faster."

"Yeah, yeah." He knew how it worked, but he still didn't like it.

"She'll be fine. You know that."

He did. Somewhere deep inside of him, he knew this kind of bite would rarely be lethal. But he couldn't shake the stark fear coursing through him. Fear over her wellbeing, her safety.

Fear he wouldn't be able to protect her when she needed him most. Hell, she'd cut her leg and gotten bit by a snake, both while on his watch.

"Hunter?"

Shit. What had Bear said? "Yeah?"

"She's getting to you," he said slowly.

Denial burned through him and he couldn't open his mouth fast enough to express it. "No way—"

"Hunter," Maya breathed.

His head snapped in her direction. "Gotta go," he said before hanging up on his boss and tossing the phone on the bench. He'd probably pay for that later, but he'd deal with it when the time came. "Hey," he said softly as he reached out and stroked her hair. "We're about to pull in."

"It hurts," she whimpered.

"I know, baby. Just a few more minutes and it'll be all gone."

He pealed into the parking lot, threw the truck in park, and got out. He had to order himself to calm down so he didn't look like a madman running into the hospital carrying a woman. He opened the door, and when he saw her struggling with the seatbelt release, he reached across her and hit the button. "C'mon," he murmured, and lifted her into his arms.

She winced, and the tiny accompanying sound was a stab to his chest. "I'm sorry," he muttered.

"The pain," she said, panting.

"I know." When he reached the front desk, he asked for the man Bear had told him to, and they were escorted to an examining room.

"Did I pass out?" she asked as he lay her on the bed.

"Not long." Her forehead was wrinkled as she squeezed her eyes shut. He just wanted to soothe her somehow, so he bent over and kissed her temple. "Relax. Breathe."

The door opened, and Hunter stood straight, almost guarding her from whoever entered. "Marco."

"What?" Hunter asked, crossing his arms. The only time he'd heard that name was in connection to the Collins crime family and Xan's ex, who was six feet under. Why the hell would this guy call him—"

"And you say *Polo*. Marco Polo. Get it?" the guy asked, smiling. "Never mind. Tough crowd." He shook his head, dropping a bag by the bed when he reached it. "I'm Sawyer." The guy walked around to the other side as he gripped his stethoscope and pulled it from his neck. "How's the patient?" he asked as he leaned closer to her. He rubbed the end of the stethoscope before resting it against her chest.

"In a shit load of pain," Hunter said, gritting his teeth, not at all amused by this man's ridiculous attempt at comedy. "You should know what's wrong. Now fix it."

Dr. Marco Polo Bullshit glanced up. "Get a grip, Anderson."

Hunter glared at him. How did this man know who he was? It made sense that Bear would've told the doctor who to meet at the hospital, but just how much had his boss relayed to a virtual stranger? Hunter sure as hell didn't like some guy he didn't know calling him by his last name.

White Coat moved around the bed again to where he'd dropped his bag. "Are you allergic to anything?" he asked Maya.

She shook her head and winced.

"Jesus, come the fuck on," he said, more than ready for her to be out of pain.

"Find your balls or get out of my exam room," the doctor ordered without taking his eyes off the patient.

Hunter growled, his temper threadbare. "I don't care what you heard about me. I'm sure it was mild compared to the truth. Don't *fuck* with me," Hunter said.

Dr. Sawyer chuckled. "I'm FBI. You don't scare me, boy." He pulled out a needle and removed the cap.

Boy? The room faded into a red haze, and he had to force himself not to tackle the S.O.B. right here. Then another thought came to him, and before it could fully process, he'd jumped over the bed and had the doc by the throat.

"Need to see some I.D, *boy,* before I let you stick her with anything."

"Hunter," Maya gasped.

"Hunter," a much louder, deeper voice said from behind him. He looked over his shoulder and saw Bear standing in the doorway. "Let. Him. Go."

Hunter looked at Sawyer, snarled at him like a rabid dog, and pushed off, effectively shoving the man in the process. The doc quickly righted himself and tugged on his white coat.

"Good to see you, Bear."

"Sawyer," Bear said with a nod.

"He smarted off and whipped out a needle. I wanted some fucking I.D." Not that Hunter needed to explain himself to anybody.

"Understood," Bear said. "But I'm here now, so you can drop the posturing bullshit. He's with the feds." He looked to the doctor whose name—first or last, he wasn't sure—was Sawyer. "And you can quit antagonizing my man."

Sawyer chuckled as he squeezed the air out of the needle, but didn't say anything else about what had just happened. Instead, he looked at Maya. "Show me that bite."

She hiked up the bottom of her stretchy pants. The doctor made a few contemplative noises as he palpated the wound, and with each touch, Maya groaned. Hunter wished the fucker would just medicate her already.

"It's definitely a snake bite."

Hunter made as if to lunge at the other man, but Bear grabbed his arm, stopping him from doing anything stupid.

Like killing him.

"I'm gonna administer an I.V. and treat you with anti-venom and morphine. Are you nauseated?"

She nodded slightly. "Helps if I keep my eyes shut."

"Then I'll give you something for that as well. Make a fist."

Hunter watched her face for any signs of distress as the doctor prepared her arm for the needle.

"Little sting. Local anesthetic."

Maya fidgeted, but didn't make a sound. Once Sawyer finished with the numbing medicine, he made quick work of the I.V. Maya gasped when it went it, and Hunter dropped to the bed, grabbed her other hand, and rubbed her cheek. "Look at me. Don't watch him."

"You're doing good."

"It burns," Maya said, panting.

Hunter gently shushed her. "He's almost finished."

"Got it," the doctor announced, and quickly taped the tube and stuff to her arm to keep it from moving. When he went into his bag again, Hunter barely paid him any attention. Instead, he zeroed in on the tears leaking from Maya's eyes, fighting the urge to kiss them away.

Sawyer injected something into Maya's I.V. port, tossed the used item into the hazardous waste bin, and retrieved another needle and vial from his bag.

"Is that it?" Maya asked as she looked at the bright orange bin on the wall and glanced at the doctor.

"No. That was the anti-venom. This,"—he raised a vial with the needle already in it—"is morphine. It'll help with the pain."

"I want her to have pills for when it wears off," Hunter said, looking at the doctor through the corner of his eye.

"Already turned it in. Script's under your name."

Hunter nodded.

"You're gonna feel this right away."

Maya bit her lip as her face pinched in obvious pain, and Hunter wished more than anything he could take the hurt away with his will alone.

"God, I hope so," she said through gritted teeth, but as

the seconds ticked by, her breathing slowed and her face became slack. Within a few minutes, she even smiled, and Hunter finally felt relief he hadn't felt since she'd gotten that damn bite.

Air whooshed out of his lungs as he looked at Sawyer. "How long does she need to stay?"

"A few hours. I need to make sure the medicine works, that she doesn't have any adverse reactions to it."

"Thanks, Sawyer, for getting here so fast," Bear said, bumping the man in the shoulder.

"No prob. I was out this way anyway."

"W-why are you *sooo* pretty?" Maya slurred, drawing the men's attention to her. When Hunter realized she was staring right at him, a shocked laugh bubbled up.

"You're high." He shook his head, smiling.

"Gotta love morphine," Sawyer said before handing a card over to Hunter. "I need to take care of a few things. Here's my number if something comes up. I'll be back in about an hour to check on her."

Hunter gave him a short nod and turned his attention back to Maya as Bear walked the doctor to the door, chatting about something. But all too soon, Bear said, "I need to speak with you."

Hunter squeezed his eyes shut, mentally preparing for the ass chewing he was about to get, and then stood. "Be right back," he whispered to Maya.

He strode past Bear, knowing his boss would follow him out into the hall. When he faced him, Hunter physically braced himself.

"You're getting too attached."

Okay, *that* wasn't what Hunter thought he was going to say. He'd figured Bear would be pissed about Maya getting hurt while on his watch. Or that Hunter had hung up on the man earlier. Not that these other words were much easier to deal with.

"I'm fine."

"You like her."

Hunter sighed. Screw it. It didn't matter if he came clean or not. "So the fuck what? I'm not doing anything about it. I haven't banged her if that's what you're worried about," he whispered heatedly. "I know protecting her is my job. I'm not going to screw it up."

Bear glanced at the door mockingly.

"Shit. Yeah, I should've been watching her better, but it's not like I let some attacker onto my property. It was a damn snake. The state's crawling with them."

His boss stared at him, and he forced himself not to flinch. Finally, he said, "Don't make me pull you off this case. Brody is neck deep in wedding planning. Blade is out of the state. That leaves Roc."

"The fuck he's coming anywhere near Maya." Hunter shook his head. "Hell no." No one would take this job from Hunter, especially not Roc.

Bear tapped his fist against Hunter's arm. "Then don't force me to make that call. The feds are all over this. It's not some private gig we got here. I know we're not working for them, but they're helping us, which means we have to be on our best behavior. You read me?"

"Loud and clear." If Bear even suspected Hunter would act on his feelings, Maya would be out of his house and he'd be back on garage duty.

Any other case, he might have preferred that. Hell, at times, he would've volunteered to switch with someone else. Before today.

Watching her get bit did something to him. He knew he couldn't have her. That didn't change, but the near-paralyzing fear awakened something in him. He couldn't trust anybody else with her safety. No one. Which meant, no way could he allow himself to give in to what was brewing with her.

She's off limits, dude, or you risk more than your job. And he heard himself.

Loud and clear.

CHAPTER TWELVE

Maya had lost track of the days since she'd gotten attacked by a vicious animal.

Okay, so vicious might be a little strong.

And she hadn't been *attacked*. She'd stepped on a snake, and it protected itself. The truth didn't help her ego any. Nor did the fact that she'd totally embarrassed herself that afternoon. She'd cried, screamed, whimpered, and passed out like a weakling. But that wasn't the worst of it. Oh no, when she screwed up, she did it big time. She'd called Hunter pretty.

To his face.

In front of his boss.

She groaned as she folded a shirt and put it in the dresser she was using in the guest room. Why had she uttered that word? She couldn't deny the man was sex personified, but she didn't have to tell him. *Gah.* Any truce she'd been trying to call the evening she'd been, um, wounded, had completely backfired. Now, instead of Hunter doing the avoiding, it was her turn.

She'd taken the baton he passed and run with it. She

could point out every crack and chipped paint on the walls of this room. Not only had she slept in here, she'd eaten in here, too. The only time she'd ventured into any other part of the house was when Hunter had knocked on her door to let her know he'd be outside in his shop for a while. Then she would slip out and watch some television.

Sighing, she grabbed the last shirt from the pile of clothes she'd cleaned, folded it, and shoved it into the drawer with the other. All that remained were panties. Rather than deal with them, she waded them up and put them in the bottom drawer. But the lacy black thong she'd worn the night everything turned to chaos taunted her from the top. She snatched them up and stormed toward the bed.

I wish I'd never met Jake.

How different her life would be right now if that was the case. She'd be in school—she looked at her watch as she bent down by the nightstand—*in psychology,* she amended as she pulled out her suitcase with more force than necessary. She didn't want the reminder of that night, the night that changed everything, so she shoved the panties as far in her bag as she could reach.

Something cut her finger, and she gasped. "Son of a bitch."

She yanked her hand out and inspected her new wound. She couldn't catch a freaking break. There was a little blood on the tip, so she sucked it as she gently peered in the bag for the culprit.

The note from Jake.

She'd gotten a paper cut from it. Jeez, he couldn't stop hurting her, could he? Well, screw him. She stormed out of the room and down the hall to the bathroom. After locking the door behind her, she stared at herself in the mirror and slowly tore the note in half.

"This is what I think of you, Jake," she sneered as she tore the pieces again. Then she wadded up the remnants and tossed the note into the trash. She slapped her hands together as if she was finally rid of him and took a deep breath. It wasn't much, but it was a start.

She still felt irritated, worked up, and really not in the mood for another workout. Glancing up as she turned to leave—to read or something—she saw the tub. *A bath.* She could take a bath, soak for a while. That would help, and it would occupy her a little bit.

She dug around the cabinets and found some Epsom salt as the water ran. She poured a generous amount into the tub, swished the water around until dissolved, then stripped. Steam rose, and she inhaled deeply before slowly stepping into the wet haven.

"Ahh." She should've done this earlier, she thought as she sat, letting the water lap over her. She could stay in here for hours.

Taking another soothing breath, she eased back even more and shut her eyes. Heaven. Pure and simple.

She opened her eyes a fraction and glanced at the trashcan. "Good riddance." Her heavy lids shut on her again, and her breathing slowed as she went boneless in the water, stress floating away as the water sluiced off her body. Within ten minutes, she was so relaxed she didn't think she could move.

That was fine. Moving was overrated anyway.

———

"DINNER'S READY," Hunter said as he knocked on the door to the guest room. He'd stayed out in the shop for the better part of the day. Not because he'd wanted to avoid

Maya—though she was the one doing most of that lately—but because he'd lost track of time, enjoying the silence of the country as he worked on the Chevelle. When he'd realized how late it was, he washed up in the garage's tiny bathroom, swung by his bedroom to change shirts, and then started on the pasta. After dinner, he'd take a real shower and try to talk the new recluse into watching a movie or something. He hadn't wanted to push her to spend time with him, but she had to be bored out of her mind. A little T.V. time wouldn't hurt anything.

When Maya didn't answer, he pounded harder.

Nothing.

"Maya?" He jiggled the doorknob in warning that he was coming in before opening the door. Why wasn't sure answering? "Maya?" he called out just a little louder after stepping into her room.

He didn't see her. Frowning, he walked toward the tiny closet, though he knew there was no way she could be in there. He had stuff crammed in it.

He checked anyway.

She wasn't there.

Panic came swiftly as he cursed and ran out of the room. He knew she wasn't in the living room because he'd walked through it earlier. She hadn't been in the kitchen, either. The light coming through the bottom of the bathroom had relief washing over him. "Thank *fuck*."

Knowing it was rude, but not really caring, he knocked on the door. "Maya, you scared the shit out of me. Dinner's ready."

No answer.

He put his ear to the door and didn't hear anything, no water running, nothing. He pounded on the door and tried twisting the locked doorknob. "Maya. This isn't funny."

Sudden splashing and violent coughing erupted.

"Fuck, fuck." He swiped his hand across the doorjamb, grabbed the key resting on the top, and shoved it in the little keyhole, quickly releasing the lock. The door crashed open as he unnecessarily put his weight against it, stumbling in.

Maya screamed and grabbed a towel to cover herself as she wheezed.

"Get out." She scrambled to get up, but only managed to get her shield soaked as she struggled to right herself in the bathtub.

Hunter growled and scooped her up. She squeaked as she tried to cover her modesty with the sopping towel. But he dropped her to her feet on the tiny rug before she could spit out an objection.

"Why were you choking?" he asked right in her face.

Her checks bloomed. "I was taking a bath and slipped under."

She was lying. Her eyes shifted. Why the hell was she lying?

Maya shoved her palm against his chest. "You had no right barging in here."

She was changing the subject. "It didn't sound like you were having a soothing bath to me."

"I—"

"Don't." He clenched her arms. "Don't you dare lie to me again, woman."

His eyes searched hers as he waited, and he watched as the fight slowly drifted out of her. "I think I fell asleep."

White-hot fury rushed through him, and it took every ounce of his will not to yell when he said, "You could have drowned."

"I-I didn't mean to. I got so relaxed that it just happened. And the pain pills make me sleepy anyway."

Jesus, he hadn't thought about her being under the influence of narcotics. Taking a bath on medication like that was beyond dangerous. She could have died.

She quickly covered his mouth with her fingertips. "Don't say it. I know it was stupid."

Very fucking stupid, but all thoughts of her carelessness fled at the sensation of her skin on his lips. He knew she hadn't meant the touch to be sensual, but that didn't stop the heat that soared through him and crackle between them in the tiny room. He knew she felt it too by the way her pupils dilated. She gasped, yanking her hand back if he'd burned her.

He didn't want her going anywhere.

Before it even registered to him that he'd moved, Hunter grabbed her delicate wrist, careful not to squeeze too tightly, stopping her retreat.

He should let her go. He needed to drop her arm and back away from her right now.

"Hunter," she breathed. The sound of his name on her lips practically destroying any sanity he was trying to wrangle. He didn't know if she was voicing a warning or an outright protest. God, he hoped it wasn't that. He wasn't sure if he could stop from tasting her again. He would if she didn't want him to, but damn, every cell in his body screamed to possess her, taste every inch of her body, lick the droplets away until the only moisture left on her was from him.

She stepped back, and he followed. There was no other choice for him. It was as if they were tethered together.

"Where are you going?" he rumbled.

She licked her lips, and he groaned.

"I–" Her back hit the wall beside the tub.

"Tell me you don't want this, that you haven't thought

about me kissing you," he said, moving closer to her, crowding her, and he lifted his arms, caging her. If she told him to stop, he would. His soul would cry out and ache, but he'd do it.

For her, he'd do anything.

He leaned closer, waiting for her answer. Her mouth opened, quivered almost with words that were not coming out. He waited, not-so-patiently, he waited, ever so slightly leaning closer still. When he couldn't stand it another second, he whispered, "Time's up," before his lips crashed to hers. He swallowed her sound of surprise as her hands flattened on his chest. She didn't push him away, though. Oh hell no, she clutched him to her, and he knew right then she'd be screaming his name before this night was over.

Grabbing her wet hair, he tilted her head and slipped his tongue into her mouth. Jesus, she tasted sweet, a flavor so unique it was both sweet and strong, like raw honey, and he immediately knew she'd be just as delectable wherever his mouth landed on her.

Just the thought of how the other parts of her body tasted had him bending slightly at the knees and thrusting between her legs as he continued to ravish her mouth. He hadn't consciously commanded his body to do so, but he knew all mental control was gone anyway. He groaned into her mouth at the contact. It felt so good he did it again and again, the intensity increasing, the pace quickly spiraling out of control. It was fast becoming not enough.

"I need inside you," he said between kisses. He needed it more than he needed the air to breathe or the sun to shine. He grabbed her leg, hiked it over his hip, and pushed against her again, the angle providing even sharper contact. His mouth landed on her neck. He needed to taste her some- where. Anywhere.

She whimpered, "Please." And *Jesus Christ,* he almost lost it then. He slammed his mouth down on hers, partly to keep her from uttering anymore words that'd have him finishing before they even started.

The towel fell or he yanked it down. He didn't know which. He didn't fucking care. His belt and pants were his next targets, needing to release his pounding cock. He was so hard it hurt, and he hissed when he was finally free.

She was naked, wet, and he was fully dressed. He couldn't remember another time when he hadn't had the patience to rid himself of his clothes, but there was a certain sexiness to the dynamic.

When she tore her mouth away, gulping in air, he still couldn't take his lips off her. He kissed down neck again, this time finding a sensitive spot behind her ear that made her shiver. Her moan only fueled him, set him on fire, delirious to wring every sound he could from her, vowing he'd never try stifling them again.

He couldn't even slow himself down enough to take in the sight of her body. He'd have to look more thoroughly later. Right now, he'd explore her in other ways.

His hand found one breast as his mouth descended on the other. And if he'd never known heaven before, he surely did now.

"Hunter," she whispered as she grabbed his head, urging him on. He didn't need the encouragement, but he loved feeling her hand in his hair. He drew on her nipple while lightly pinching and tugging the other. She came up on her toes, beautifully whispered begs falling from her lips.

"God, your taste," he muttered against her skin after releasing her and trekking south, kissing and nipping at her ribs, her bellybutton, until he reached her mound. She trembled as he rubbed his nose along the small patch of curls, waiting.

She didn't have to wait long. Without warning, he grabbed her knee, threw her leg over his shoulder, and buried his face in her pussy. He knew he should have teased her, made her want it until she was mindless of anything else but what heights of passion he could give her, but he was so lost in her essence, her flavor, that he could do nothing but devour her. He licked, sucked, and stabbed his tongue into her. She squirmed, practically vibrating with need, and he had to place a hand on her tummy to keep her from losing her balance.

He had more important things to do with the other one.

His free hand slipped between her legs, and he allowed one finger to penetrate her. Just one. It was all he needed. Crooking his finger, he rubbed the spot behind her clit from within as his mouth circled it and his tongue batted relentlessly against the hard nub.

"Oh my god. Oh my god," she began to chant as her hand fisted painfully in his hair, only able to grab pieces of it since it was so short. But within seconds, the words coming from her mouth became incoherent as she screamed, her pussy fisting around his finger. Feeling her cream on his hand was one of the most glorious things he'd ever felt in his life, but he knew that was about to change.

Waiting for her to come down was torture, but somehow, he managed to find the strength. When she was panting and going limp, he scooped her into his arms.

No protest came from her as he whisked her down the hall and into his bedroom.

Once he placed her on his bed, he made quick work of stripping out of his clothes and climbing onto the bed with her. No words were exchanged as he fished out a condom from his nightstand and rolled it on. He was so fucking eager to be inside of her he almost couldn't stand it. He climbed on top of her, ready to possess every inch of her, but even in his haste, he found the strength to hesitate at her entrance.

"Tell me now if you don't want this."

"Don't stop." She shook her head, and that was all he needed to hear. "Please, I need—*ahh.*" He thrust into her, taking her, fucking her with every part of his being. His grip was so tight on her shoulder and hip that he knew he'd be leaving bruises.

He didn't know where this deep-rooted need for her was coming from. No matter how hard he tried, he couldn't get close enough, deep enough. That didn't stop him from trying.

"So good," he growled, and slammed into her harder.

His name rent the air as she squeezed the ever-lovin' shit out of him. He wasn't going to last. Hell, it was a struggle to keep thrusting into her, she was so tight.

"Oh, *god,*" she groaned, and he could feel just how much wetter she got as she clamped down on his dick. "Yes," she screamed.

"Fuck, baby. Come all over me." He reared up on his knees and grabbed her thighs to keep her from sliding away with the force of his thrusts, all without stopping his torment. She'd come down from her high, but she still clung to him, greedy for more, and he'd give her everything she wanted. He held her there in his iron grip as he plowed into her over and over and over again.

"Please, oh god, please," she begged as she slapped her hands against the headboard, pushed herself even closer to him, and arched her back, making him reach depths he'd never even dreamed were possible. Her perfect breasts bounced with each penetrative push. It was all almost too much. He threw his head back and groaned, squeezing his eyes shut, his neck straining with effort, as he fought his orgasm just a little bit longer.

Within moments, he got what he wanted as she screamed incoherent words, her body shaking with the force of her climax, and still he didn't slow his pace. He was past the point of no return, taking her with a savage need.

"Oh, fuck, fuck." He fell over her again, gripping the headboard beside her hand, and pounded into her, harder, deeper, practically fucking her into the mattress, its bounce working with him as he fed this primal pent-up need.

"Hunter," she moaned, and he snapped at the erotic sound of his name on her pleasure-consumed lips.

"Take it, baby," he said right before roaring out his release. He kept pumping into her, unable to stop himself as he kept coming, drawing out the peak of passion for as long as he could.

When the intense pleasure began to lessen, he finally slumped over her, sucking air into his heaving lungs.

"Goddamn," he breathed.

His muscles screamed, and sweat trickled down his back from the force of his effort, but that wasn't the only thing he felt there–her hands.

Gentle fingertips trailed lazy circles along his spine, and somehow, that minor touch did more to his heart than the mind-blowing sex they'd just had.

Lifting up, he looked at her. Really looked at her. Maya's skin was pale, save for the red splotches he'd created and a few freckles here and there.

"You're so beautiful," he whispered before kissing her. Lightly. Reverently. She slipped her hands up his back and returned the kiss with the same meaning-filled emotion he was giving.

Already he felt the tingle at the base of his spine, his body trying to ready himself for another go. No way would it happen right now. Not yet anyway, but never before had the need been there so soon after spending himself. What was it about this woman? He didn't know.

As he continued to kiss her slowly, he knew he was almost too scared to find out.

Almost?

He was scared shitless.

CHAPTER THIRTEEN

THE SUN SHINING through the window woke Hunter, but
he was already smiling before he opened his eyes. The last
several days had been nothing but laughing, eating, fucking,
and sleeping. He couldn't remember the last time he'd had
this much fun with a woman.

Or the last time he let one sleep in his bed. Yeah, it'd
happened before. He wasn't one of those assholes who
kicked a girl out after sex, but usually, he tried working his
way into their houses, not bringing them home to his. But
Maya was stuck here.

Lately, he hadn't minded.

The morning after he'd walked in on her in the shower
might've been weird if he'd allowed it, but he'd fucked her
well into the night. She'd been too exhausted to allow any
embarrassment or whatever girly feelings were normal after
having sex with a man for the first time. He'd slapped her on
the butt and instructed her to get up to help him with breakfast. When she'd shyly helped pull out food from the fridge,
he'd laid her on the table, taken the orange juice, and spilled

it between her legs. She'd laughed and playfully fought until he'd began lapping it up around her clit.

After breakfast, they'd showered and had sex again. Pretty much the pattern for the last couple of days.

He rubbed his hand where she'd recently been beside him. The bed was still warm there, so she hadn't been gone long. Tossing the covers to the side, he got up, not bothering to put on underwear, and walked out. He was going to head to the kitchen, hoping she'd put on some coffee, but he heard the shower running in the bathroom and turned in that direction instead. He smirked when he twisted the knob and found the door unlocked.

Stepping lightly, he made his way to the shower, quietly wincing at her horrible singing. Jesus, she couldn't carry a tune in a bucket, but at least it kept her distracted as he grabbed a condom from the drawer.

He pushed open the curtain. "Just how I like my women. Naked."

"Hunter," she gasped, covering her luscious breasts. He stepped in and pulled her hands free.

"Don't hide from me, baby."

"Did you not learn your lesson the last time you scared me while I was in here?"

"Mmm...I enjoyed *that* lesson."

She swatted him. "Perv."

His mouth descended on hers without any warning. She giggled at the suddenness, but any humor died as she began moaning. It was all he could do to get the condom open and on without breaking away from her. He pushed her against the wall, urging her to wrap her legs around him, and he sent a silent prayer up when she did. He didn't know where his control was. He'd lost it days ago, but somehow, he'd found the willpower to rub against her, making sure she was as turned on as he was, while shielding her from the shower.

"Stop teasing me," she breathed.

He smiled as he kissed down her neck and back up to her ear. "You like the things I do to you."

Before she could respond, he thrust into her partway. She gasped and clawed at his shoulders as he pulled almost completely out and pushed all the way in.

"Fuck, but you feel so good," he groaned, and began to move inside her.

She muttered something he couldn't make out. He wasn't sure if it was because of the blood rushing in his head, making it impossible to hear, or if she wasn't being coherent. Either way, it didn't matter. He was too focused on this, on her.

One of her hands tangled in his short hair, and she bit the side of his neck as she gyrated against him. It was so damn sexy the way she tried taking control when he was the one holding her, fucking her, but he knew how to take the reins back. He slipped a hand between them and lightly grazed her clit. She threw her head back, banging the tile. "*Yes.*"

"You like that?" he taunted as he barely stroked her. She groaned and tried following his finger when he retreated, but he held her still. "I asked you a question," he said, tapping her clit as he fucked her.

"Oh god."

"My name's Hunter, though I understand your confusion." He chuckled, enjoying her torment and not letting up on it either.

"Yes," she said, frustrated. "I like it."

Another gentle swipe. Another gasp. Now she was quivering and he knew it wasn't because she was about to come. It was because she wanted to. "Tell me what you like. Specifically, Maya."

She whimpered and rotated her hips, trying to increase the friction where she wanted it. He moved his hand and pelvis away so she wouldn't find any relief until she complied.

He swooped down and sucked a nipple into his mouth. She moaned and held him to her.

"All you have to do is tell me, and I'll do it, baby. Just tell me. Tell me with that dirty little mouth of yours what you want." He switched to the other nipple and tongued it rapidly.

"*Ahh*. I...I want you to make me come." She panted now.

"How?"

Her scream was pure frustration, and he had to hold back a laugh.

"I want you to finger me fast and fuck me hard."

All playfulness vanished at her words. His mouth slammed down on hers again. His finger flew over her hard little clit, and he plowed into her so hard, he wasn't sure if he was going to last.

Tearing his mouth away, he said, "Come on, baby. Come for me." He increased the pressure of his finger and held his cock still deep inside of her.

"Oh god, oh god. Don't stop. Don't–" She screamed as her pussy fisted him. He grabbed both of her ass cheeks and fucked her hard and deep, thrusting several more times until he was roaring out his own release.

The cool water stung his back, and his groan turned into a chuckle. "Jesus, woman, how long were you in here? Water's gettin' cold."

"Part of the time is your fault," she muttered into his shoulder.

He pulled away, wincing as his dick slid free, and helped her to her feet. "Gotta hurry before it gets colder than a polar bear's ass in here."

She giggled. "I'm done. Or was." She quickly rewashed and rinsed before gripping the curtain.

"Hold up," he said as he grabbed her arm. She turned a puzzled look at him over his shoulder, and fuck him, but that look was just as sexy as any other she'd tossed his way. Shaking the thought off, he said, "We're going to the shop."

Her eyes popped. "You mean we get to leave the grounds? No one will be waiting with handcuffs to haul me back here if I try to leave with you?"

He swatted her bare ass and she squealed, jumping out of the tub. He pulled the curtain to the side, ignoring the cold water, and watched as she dried herself. "Very funny. You're not a prisoner here, though I can definitely arrange those handcuffs if you want."

"Forget it." She narrowed her eyes, and he winked at her.

"Seriously, though, I have a meeting. Instead of getting the intel secondhand, I'd rather just go. We haven't had any issues, so I don't see the problem going in for an hour or two."

"Yay." She clapped her hands and darted out of the bathroom, acting as if he'd told her they were going to Vegas or something. He suppressed a laugh and tipped his head under the showerhead. He cursed at the near-freezing water and turned the hot water all the way on. It didn't help much, but when he saw a soapy handprint on the wall where he'd just pinned Maya and images of fucking her flooded his mind, he figured the temperature wouldn't matter anyway.

He was going to need that cold shower after all.

———

MAYA NEVER THOUGHT she'd find riding in a beat-up truck so exhilarating. The trees zoomed by as gravel road turned to asphalt, and all too soon they were crossing into Mayflower city limits and pulling into the Bang Shift Garage.

"What does that name even mean?" she asked as Hunter parked.

He smiled. "It's car-geek slang for shifting a manual transmission pretty fast."

"Oh, like a four banger? I've heard that before, somewhere."

"Not exactly. That's an engine with four cylinders. But it's all grease monkey talk." She opened her mouth, and he put his hand up, chuckling. "That means mechanic. C'mon, college girl, you can learn more later." He wagged his eyebrows and got out. Before she had a chance to open her door, he clutched her arm, pulled her across the bench seat, and helped her out through the driver's side.

"I could've gotten out—"

"Look," he started, his gaze shifting to the shop, his easy smile dropping. "What's happening between us. I want to keep it between us. Understand?" He stepped back, probably putting no more than an inch of space between them, but it felt as if it were miles. Her heart ached, and she mentally blasted herself for letting things get this far. He was a bad boy. Of course he didn't want her flaunting their fling. He was probably too worried about his image.

He growled—like seriously growled—at her. "Whatever you're thinking, stop that shit right now," he whispered heatedly. "I work with these guys. I don't want to be ragged on. Not that it'd have anything to do with you," he added quickly as she felt the blood drain from her face. Was he embarrassed by her? "Fuck, this isn't coming out right. It's just none of their business. Okay?"

"Fine." She turned and walked toward the garage, though she felt anything but fine. She felt like a used piece of garbage. Why she expected Hunter to be any different, she didn't know.

Because you like him, that's why. Why were men such mean morons?

"We're talking about this later," he said as he caught up with her and opened the door to the shop before she could.

She didn't respond.

"Well, look what the pus—I mean, cat dragged in," the guy with dark hair said. She couldn't remember his name. He hadn't talked much the other night.

"Shut up, Roc," Hunter said, and this Roc man winked at her. Yeah, that was a little creepy.

"Told you it wasn't necessary for you to come in," Bear said as he walked into the open area they were standing in by the lobby. He smiled at her then. "Hi, Maya."

"Hello."

"We both needed to get out for a few. No big deal." Hunter shrugged.

Bear nodded. "Brody's heading in. Should be here any minute."

The two guys continued to talk, but their voices drifted away as she saw something in the garage.

Up in the air.

"Is that my car?" she asked, walking toward it without thinking.

"Yes," Bear said.

But why was it up there? The last time she saw it, it was a mangled mess—and in Texas. Besides, she couldn't afford to get it fixed. Not without telling her parents or dipping into her savings. Even if she did that, her parents would know.

She had just opened her mouth to explain this—again— when the door dinged.

"Sorry we're late," Brody said. He flashed a smile at her as he held the door open.

"We?" Bear asked.

"Hey," Xan said as she walked in with Roxie. The other woman smiled and waved, but quickly dropped her hand when she looked at Bear. She didn't understand why she'd do that. She and Xan seemed friendly when they'd visited with her before.

Bear shifted his gaze, as though he couldn't even look at Roxie.

"Let's get started," he said to Hunter. "Gauge is on a run, so he won't be here for this."

"Wait," Xan said, moving quickly over to Bear. "I was thinking we could take Maya to Little Rock to shop for some wedding decorations." Xan smiled and nodded at Maya before looking at Bear again.

It wasn't the big bald man who spoke. "Absolutely not," Hunter said.

"No way," Brody said at the same time. "Is that why you wanted to come up here? I told you I'd pick you and Roxie up when I got finished and take you wherever you wanted to go."

"She can't go without protection," Hunter said with a

strange air of finality. It irritated her that he acted all protective now when just a few minutes ago he was ready to pretend she didn't matter to him.

"Why?" Roxie asked, looking at each of the men, saving Bear for last. When no one answered, she stomped over to the big bald man and got in his face.

Got. In. His. Face.

The woman was like half his height and no bigger than a minute, but she stared down the behemoth as if he was as harmless as a ant.

Bear gritted his teeth and his body grew stiff as stone as he stood there in silence. "Why can't she go, huh? There has been nothing going on. Nothing. You're all are acting ridiculous. My cousin said there hasn't been anything–"

"Flint doesn't know shit," Bear roared.

Maya jumped and then inched behind Hunter. From the looks on everyone's faces, they were as shocked as she was. Well, everyone except Roxie. That woman hadn't even flinched when Bear yelled. She'd been irritated before, but now she looked downright pissed. If looks could kill, Bear would be in a bloody heap on the floor.

No one made a sound as the two of them glared at each other, which sort of freaked her out. It was as if no one even dared to breathe. The tension was so thick it was palpable. Maya didn't know them very well, but it was obvious this wasn't really about her.

Roxie shook her head and started to turn away.

"Don't walk away from me!" The command was so forceful Maya had to keep herself from walking to him.

Roxie, though, she just laughed without any humor as she glanced over her shoulder at him. "You can get over yourself, or you can fuck straight off. I don't even care anymore." With that, Roxie tossed her fiery red hair over her shoulder as she gave him her back. She faced Xan and said, "I'mma be in the car," before storming off.

When Maya looked at Bear again, his face was red and his hands were fisted at his sides.

"I'm going with them," Brody said, obviously not sticking around for the meeting. When Maya looked at him, he'd put his arm around Xan. He shook his head lightly at her when it looked as if she was about to object. "You can fill me in later," he said to Bear, not taking his eyes off his soon-to-be wife.

Bear didn't say anything before he turned and walked off. The door slamming behind him made her jump again.

"He's normally not like that," Hunter muttered. "Like ever."

Maya swallowed the questions. She didn't know that man, so she couldn't say either way if he was or not. Regardless, she had no right to be noisy.

"I'll watch her closely," Brody said, and gave a nod in Maya's direction, leaving no question who he was talking about.

Hunter's gaze shot to him. "She stays here. With me."

Well, now...for a man who didn't want his co-workers knowing how he felt about her, he was sure acting like he gave a care. What happened to him being quick to tell her to keep quiet about their relationship? *And that was after screwing my brains out.* Maya stepped back and glared at him.

"Last time I checked, you weren't my dad. Or my boyfriend," she said just low enough for him to hear. She looked at Xan. "I'd love to go."

The other woman smiled.

"Maya," Hunter said, a warning in his tone. She didn't care. It wasn't as if she was running away with the girls without protection. Brody said he'd watch her, and the dude was huge. What did it matter who did the babysitting as long as there was some big ogre within arm's reach?

"Hunter," she said in a sickeningly sweet voice. She figured that Roxie chick had left some badass estrogen in the air and Maya all too eagerly sucked it all up. Without another word, she quickly made her way to the door.

"I got it," Brody said, but she didn't catch anything else because the door had shut between them.

She walked to the car with a new sense of freedom. The trees and such were nice earlier, but now she was going to get out for real.

As she reached the late-model Honda, she saw Roxie sitting in the back, looking out with glazed eyes.

Maya approached the car slowly so she didn't freak the other woman out. When she opened the door and eased in beside her, Roxie blinked a few times, but didn't look at her.

Jeez, Xan must like vanilla. The car reeked of it.

Finally, Roxie said, "Don't ever fall in love."

Maya looked at her, wondering if she should ask her to explain. That one sentence could mean so much. Instead, she said the only thing she honestly could. "I wish it was that simple."

"It never is," Roxie said. "Never."

And to that, Maya had nothing else to add.

CHAPTER FOURTEEN

BEAR'S KNEE was bouncing when Hunter walked in with Roc in tow.

"Flint Willis," Bear growled, shaking his head as the guys took a seat. Hunter knew Flint and Bear had long been friends before something massive happened between the two of them.

"Flint doesn't matter right now," Hunter said, trying to diffuse whatever was going on in Bear's head. He knew since his boss had never talked about it before, he wasn't going to now. That wasn't to say he'd never open up about whatever went down, but Bear was too much of a stickler for rules to do it on company time. Besides, Hunter needed the guy to focus on their current predicament, not dwell on whatever went sour with his former friend.

His boss shut his eyes and took a deep breath. Then another. "You're right. I'm sorry."

After he got that out, he looked up, and Hunter could almost see the guy pushing his issues away. The leg under the table quit bouncing. Bear's jaw relaxed.

"We don't have anything really new. The feds have

picked apart Oberman. They can't find anything else other than he's one of Rudolph's soldiers. He's a nobody in that organization. Hell, other than knowing Oberman works for him, there's no other record of the two even knowing each other."

"Happens," Roc said, shrugging. "One of his lieutenants could've hired him. Rudolph might not even recognize Oberman if he saw the kid on the street."

Hunter shook his head. "No way. I don't buy it. Oberman weaseled his way into my sister's life for a reason. Rudolph is a smart man. He'd have covered his tracks."

"And we know that, too," Bear said, cutting his gaze back to Hunter. "That's why we and the feds have looked at this from every angle. Oberman has never been photographed at any meetings with Rudolph. And the last time Rudolph was in Texas, Oberman was in New Mexico on summer break, so we can't even put them in the same state at the same time."

"That's what phones, e-mail, the Internet, all that is for. A webcam and a connection is all you need to see people nowadays."

"His calls are monitored," Roc said.

Hunter's head whipped around. "Don't give me that shit. We both know there are ways around that."

"Obviously, which is why our guys with the Bureau have been working around the clock to find the link. As of right now, there is none."

"So what happens now?" Hunter asked with eyes narrowed. He had a feeling he wasn't going to like the answer.

Bear sighed. "She can't go anywhere until we get her car fixed; with the exception of Parsons, our contacts within the FBI are ready to back down. Without their support, her parents would easily find out she's not at school or away on a project. And that would be a game changer. I say we keep digging until her car's fixed."

"And then?" Hunter knew, but he wanted Bear to say the words.

"She goes back to school, man. And Blade comes home. We move on."

Leave his sister alone to fend for herself? No fucking way. "I'm not leaving Heather unprotected."

"You can't stick her in your pocket and keep her there." Bear threw up his hands. "What if this is just a case of some little shit getting pissed off for being dumped? How much time and resources have to be spent before it's enough for you?"

"When that prick gets thrown in jail."

"No." Bear's fist dropped to the table, slamming it. "That could take years. You know that. I need you to get your head outta your ass and think. Step away from it emotionally and look at this case like you would normally —*objectively*."

Hunter groaned and rubbed his face. He knew his boss was right, but he didn't want to admit that. Not yet. Instead of facing those facts, he asked, "How much longer do we have?"

"Roc?" Bear asked, raising an eyebrow.

"Fender came in yesterday, front bumper today. Other dents were able to be knocked out. All the glass has been replaced. Even put new tires on it since the tread was low. Should be ready in a few days, I think."

"So by the weekend. She could be back in classes by Monday. You'll have to let go then," he added softly.

Monday. He wanted to argue, but knew it wouldn't work. He *was* going to have to let her go, and he didn't know the first thing about how to go about doing that. He glanced at Bear to see if his boss was waiting for a response, but the man wasn't looking at him. He stared across the room, and Hunter caught something moving under the table. Bear's knee. What was his boss thinking about now? He had a feeling it didn't have anything to do with the case.

And everything to do with letting someone go.

Hunter would be willing to bet his house that Bear was thinking about Roxie. It was obvious something had happened between the two of them, and whatever it was left unresolved feelings.

Was that what Hunter had to look forward to? Letting go of a woman for reasons that might seem right only to live life in regret? In pain?

He didn't want that. But what could he do? Fuck, he didn't know. But the more he thought about Maya, one thing was becoming painfully clear.

He cared for her more than he ever wanted to. More than he ever wanted to care for any woman. What was he supposed to do with that? Let go of the woman he loved?

Whoa. Love? He pushed the chair back and got up from the table without looking at the other two men. He couldn't. He knew the emotional questions would be reflected in his eyes. Did he love her? Could he?

Those questions were burning in him, but another one demanded his attention. One he was ashamed to admit.

Did it even matter?

Yes, that made him a bastard, but the question was there anyway, taunting him, searing him deep in his chest. Did it matter if he loved her?

When he'd just let her go anyway.

———

MAYA CARRIED the bags up the porch to Hunter's house. She shouldn't have bought the new clothes, but once she'd gotten to the mall with the girls, her natural female instincts had kicked in. Retail therapy had been exactly what she needed. She immersed herself in jeans and shoes and didn't think about much else. Xan and Roxie had been a lot of fun, too, hamming it up with her. The three also got a kick out of Brody's discomfort when it came to the wedding registry. Maya had never had that much fun shopping before.

Of course, when she'd pulled her wallet out to pay for the first pair of shoes she'd snagged, Brody had insisted on taking care of the bill. At first, she hadn't understood, but then Xan had whispered something about not needing to leave a paper trail. The fact the woman knew so quickly must've been a sign of how in tune she was with her fiancé. That, or Xan knew more about the worries of leaving behind evidence than she should. Maya didn't know which, but she hoped it was the first reason.

After they finished shopping, Brody drove through a frozen custard place, and Maya wondered where the sweet goodness had been all her life. That stuff put ice cream to shame.

Now stuffed with yummy junk food and toting a few new things for her wardrobe, she returned to Hunter's feeling better than when she'd last seen him. Nothing was resolved between them, but she was better prepared now.

It had to be the sugar.

When she reached the door, Hunter opened it before she could. He waved at the car, and Brody threw up a peace sign before backing out. Maya waved quickly before the car turned and drove off.

Hunter took the bags from her. "Looks like you had fun."

She followed him inside and shut the door. "I did. It was nice getting out. Amazing how someone can watch you without making you feel like a prisoner." She smiled sweetly as she kicked off her sneakers.

He put the bags down. "I deserved that."

"You deserve more than that," she muttered, and turned away from him. He reached for her, stopping her retreat.

"What do I deserve?" he asked, his nose grazing through her hair. He slowly trailed his hand up and down her arm.

"You're not being fair," she breathed.

"I don't play fair. Not when it comes to you."

Her head fell back onto his chest, and he slowly wrapped an arm around her waist.

"I didn't mean to hurt your feelings earlier," he whispered into her ear. Then he sucked the lobe between his lips and nibbled it. "I'm sorry."

She groaned. "Why do you know what to say to make me want you?"

"Do you want me?" he asked, and she didn't miss his erection when he plastered himself against her back.

"Yes," she said, unable to keep the answer from coming out.

He gently tilted her head and kissed her neck. She could stand here like this forever, feeling his mouth on her. She didn't know why she loved it so much, why this man pulled this kind of response from her...

And she had no way of stopping her reaction to him.

She'd discovered that the first time he'd taken her. She'd been shocked to find him busting through the bathroom door, but any irritation had gone bye-bye with one look into his smoldering eyes. He'd wanted her, too, and there wasn't anything hotter than a sexy man's need being so clearly displayed. Did it make it right? No. In the back of her mind, she knew she'd regret this eventually, had even started to earlier.

But being near him disintegrated all negative thoughts. It made her weak, but only for him, and right now, she was okay with that.

More than okay.

"I want to take all your clothes off, kiss you everywhere, and have you begging for more," he said as he tugged her shirt off one shoulder and peppered her with his kisses.

He might as well knock her to her ass because his words were making her weak in the knees anyway. It took more strength than she thought she had to pull away from him and turn to face him, and not because she didn't want this.

She almost smiled at his confused look.

She might be totally gone for this man, but no way would she be the only one begging when it came to sex. It was time he got a taste of his own medicine. If she felt entitled to a little payback because of how he'd acted earlier, she ignored it. She didn't want anything tainting this time but good, clean fun.

Good, clean, torturous fun.

She reached for his belt and slowly unbuckled it. When she glanced up at him, her serious expression almost cracked at his partial smile. She maintained eye contact with him as she unfastened his jeans and slowly pulled the zipper down.

His smile vanished.

He gritted his teeth to the point his jaw flexed, and he stood still, waiting.

Good.

As she pushed his pants and boxer-briefs down, she dropped to her knees.

He groaned softly, probably realizing what she was about to do, and widened his stance a little bit.

Not much for preliminaries, she licked the head of his penis. He gasped at the contact and gripped her hair, not tightly, but enough to know he held her.

She sucked him into her mouth, and had to put her hands on his thighs for balance. They stiffened beneath her palms, and her nails dug in slightly as she took him as far in as she could.

"Yes," he hissed. He wadded her hair into a makeshift ponytail in one hand and caressed her cheek with the other. "So good."

Maya had never felt she was any good at this. Even figured it probably didn't matter much anyway. But there was no denying the truth in Hunter's praise.

Feeling more secure, she let go of one of his thighs and eased her hand between his legs. When she tugged on his balls, he gasped and thrust into her mouth.

Groaning, he said, "Sorry," and straightened. She didn't want that. She wanted him weak and needy, yes, but she also wanted him to be free to react however he needed.

She let him slip free and she stroked him as she looked up. "Don't apologize. Do whatever you want."

The hand in her hair tightened as his eyes got darker. "I just want to enjoy this until you're ready to stop."

"Liar." She smiled. Fine. If he wanted to play like that, then they would. The gloves were coming off.

She sucked him back into her mouth, keeping a hand on the root to stroke him as her head bobbed. She also kept her other hand on his balls and played with them. There was no going easy. She jacked him hard as her tongue tortured his glans. His thighs shook, and every once in a while, a curse would fall from his lips.

Jeez, he had killer stamina, but as she worked him, she could feel his control slipping. The grip on her hair would tighten. He'd barely thrust before checking himself.

She thought about talking dirty to him, but she wasn't that brave.

His flavor darkened a little, and she moaned around him at the taste.

"Fuck," he growled, and yanked her up. He turned her, grabbed her waist, took three steps to the couch, and bent her over the back of it. "That was goddamn torture." He whipped her pants down.

Unable to stop, she giggled at her victory.

"You think that's funny?" A condom wrapper ripped.

"I think it's payback."

"Famous last words, baby."

He drove into her from behind, taking her with a force that had her rising up on her toes. He thrust hard and fast, and she was so turned on from pleasing and teasing him that she was already about to come. Words fell from her mouth as she rocked back against him, meeting him each time.

Stars exploded behind her eyelids as she screamed his name, orgasming harder than she ever had before.

And still he didn't stop.

When her throat grew sore and she slumped, depleted, he wrapped his arms around her midsection and hoisted her up. She was still pinned to the couch, but now his mouth was at her ear.

"I can fuck you hard and fast or nice and slow." He demonstrated the latter by sensually easing in and out of her. "Sometimes you need to get fucked like that. Other times, you need to be made love to...like this." He kissed her ear as he continued the leisurely pace, his panting breath punctuated with moans.

He was making love to her. Love. Somehow, what had been the hardest sex of her life was now the most meaning-ful. How could this man do that to her? Have that kind of effect on her?

She gasped when he slipped his hand under her shirt and squeezed her breast. Her head tipped back, and he slipped his hand between her legs, trailing lazy circles around her clit.

"I feel you everywhere," he whispered, and she knew he didn't mean physically.

At least she wasn't in this thing alone. She didn't even want to like him, care about him, but she'd never thought about loving him.

Heat rushed to her face. Oh god, she did love him. She gasped, and he misunderstood why because he increased his pace. But now that his thrusts and his finger were going faster, she realized she was close to coming. This man was making love to her, and she was about to have another orgasm, one completely different, but so much more. Maybe he *hadn't* misunderstood anything at all.

Maybe he'd been able to read her from the beginning.

"Maya," he breathed. "I–" He dug his head into her shoulder and groaned.

What was he going to say? The thought that he might be struggling to confess his feelings had her tingling all over. He pushed into her harder, and she gasped. "Oh, god."

He didn't increase his pace, just kept slamming into the same spot inside of her, bursts of electricity igniting each time.

"What the?" She was confused and so incredibly turned on. He was still plowing into her, but now he needed the force because she was fisting him so tightly.

"That's it," he crooned. "Give it to me, baby. I'm close. I want you with me. Always with me."

She was too far gone to read anything more into his words than how they applied to the present. Unable to stand it anymore, she pushed back, taking him as deep as she could, and rotated her hips, keeping him inside.

"Oh, fuck," he breathed, clenching her hip, probably trying to still her so he wouldn't come, but she was already dangling on that precipice, about to fly over the edge.

"Hunter," she said, and moved faster. White-hot ecstasy engulfed her just as he shouted, coming at the same time.

With her.

It was long moments later before either of them got their wits back. And when they were both back in reality, no weirdness came.

He kissed her neck and guided her to the bathroom where he washed her body slowly and kissed her gently many times. It was a different kind of lovemaking.

Because she loved him. God help her, she did.

CHAPTER FIFTEEN

"Shit." Oil leaked from under the Chevelle and almost hit Hunter in the eye. *Fucking chrome pan.* Next on the to-do list was to replace that sucker. He wiped his face and rolled from under the car.

He'd spent all morning double-checking intel they'd gotten from the feds on Jake Oberman. He hadn't been able to come up with any solid connection to Alonzo other than he was one of the man's lackeys. That didn't tell him squat. If he didn't find something soon, Maya would be going back to Texas and his sister would be left to fend for herself.

Now, instead of worrying about one woman, he feared for two. It wasn't a feeling he was comfortable with at all, which was why he'd burned the midnight oil researching... then fueled working on the car with this morning's coffee. Tinkering with American metal always helped him find his balance. He'd missed working on this car, especially.

But he'd trade it all, never touch another car again, if it meant Maya and Heather would be okay.

He wiped his hands as he stood, cleaning the grease out

from under his nails. He checked the system on his wrist and noticed nothing had been tripped, though he'd have heard the alarms if something was wrong. He looked at the house monitors again and found Maya reading. He smiled at how serious she looked. She was probably studying. She spent her free time making sure she wasn't behind in any of her classes.

Because she'd have to go back to school.

He threw the cloth down and cursed. He knew she'd have to go back, but something didn't feel right. He didn't know what it was, but it was there, eating away at him.

"I knew I'd find a weakness in your system."

Hunter whirled. Gauge stood there, Bear and Brody to his right, holding the bypass box he'd told his team about. Brody had used it a few times, but usually, the other guys alerted him when they were coming over.

"You could've knocked," Hunter said, his gaze moving from Gauge to Bear to Brody. "What the fuck are you all doing here?" And why was Roc manning the garage alone?

"We found the link," Bear said, grim. "It's bad."

Hunter wiped his hands on the bottom of his tank and crossed his arms. "What?" he asked, bracing himself. He glanced at the screen, but did a double take. Someone was moving in one of the rooms. He rushed to the monitor, ready to bolt out of the garage and into the house to save Maya, but he could identify that messy mop of black hair anywhere. "The fuck is Roc doing in my house?" He glared at Bear.

"Sweeping."

"For bugs?" Hunter asked incredulously. "First of all, no one has gotten past me." He pointed to Gauge. "Taking apart my hidden shit that even military-grade sensors couldn't find doesn't count."

"I'll give you that," Gauge said, not smiling.

"And second, my system would detect a foreign surveillance apparatus." He didn't like Roc much anyway. The man would be the last Hunter would pick to rifle through his things.

"That may be, but I want to be sure," Bear said. "Because someone *has* gotten past you."

"Who?" he barked.

"Maya."

Hunter blinked, not sure he'd heard correctly. "Come again?"

"Dude," Brody said as he walked toward Hunter. He didn't like that look on his friend's face. In fact, the air was already going thin. "We were looking for any connections between Maya Carmichael and Jake Oberman and between Oberman and Alonzo Rudolph."

"But we weren't looking for any links directly between Rudolph and Maya," Bear added.

Hunter's body grew cold. "Explain."

The garage door creaked, drawing all of their attention. Roc walked in, carrying torn pieces of paper.

"When's the last time you took out your trash?" Roc asked, nose wrinkled.

"Did you find anything?" Bear asked, waving him in.

"Negative. No tracking devices or anything like that. But I did find this note addressed to Maya in the bathroom trashcan. It reads, 'You know what I want, *criado*.'"

"What the hell?" Hunter said, shaking his head. That couldn't be right. No way.

"I thought it might be important, since she tore it up, but I couldn't be sure. You know what it means?" Roc asked.

All eyes were on Hunter, but all he could do was shake his head. "No fucking way." But it wasn't an answer.

"What, man?" Brody asked, and grabbed his arm, trying to get his attention and failing. Hunter couldn't look at him, at any of them. How could she know about that? There was no way. Unless...

"You want proof that Rudolph and Oberman were connected. There's your proof." He pointed to the pieces of the letter. "*Criado* is what Rudolph called me. Oberman had to know that." But why use the whole phrase like Alonzo always had? Hunter frowned, trying to piece the puzzle together.

"What does that mean?"

"Servant," Roc said, and Hunter's gaze flashed to him. "What?" Roc asked, defiant.

"He's right," Hunter finally said, and began to pace. "It's what Rudolph called me. I was his servant. He wanted me to follow orders without question."

"That doesn't mean anything," Brody said. When Hunter faced him, he continued, "He could call *all* his people that, including Oberman. If Oberman is twisted, maybe he called Maya that, pretending it was something sweet. As far as she knows, it could be a term of endearment."

"He's right," Gauge said. "The note doesn't prove anything, but this does." He held up a sheet of paper.

"What's that?" Hunter asked, walking toward him.

"Printout of bank activity. When Maya was eighteen, money was wired into her savings account from a small company that has been bought and sold many times. But if you follow the trail, they all lead to one of Alonzo Rudolph's shell companies."

"So Rudolph paid her," Roc said, sneering.

"When she was old enough to be at college," Gauge continued.

"Which was when she met your sister," Bear said.

Hunter spun, fisting his hands. Did that mean—

"Sorry, man," Brody said. "Looks like Rudolph was after you all along and was going through your sister to get to you."

"Then why not do it sooner?" he asked, though he shouldn't have had to. He knew Alonzo well enough to know the man wouldn't strike until he'd cause the most damage. Like when he'd gotten Hunter to fall in love with a woman Alonzo controlled. He'd played right into that freak's hands.

And Maya had played him from the beginning.

Jesus, he was going to be sick.

"Heather," he breathed, and practically leapt in front of Bear. "I have to get to her." She wasn't safe there, and she wouldn't understand why. Hell, when he explained, she would probably defend her roommate's actions with some crazy reason.

Bear pulled out his phone. "I left a message for Blade earlier to check in. He hasn't yet, but I'll have them catch the first flight out." When Blade didn't answer, Bear left a message stating the three of them were to fly out as soon as possible.

"Blade hasn't checked in?" Brody said, frowning.

"He won't risk his cover," Gauge said, waving him off.

"Calm down," Bear said. "He made his morning call. I've heard from him every time he's supposed to. Anna, too. I left a message after getting this new intel."

That wasn't good enough. "No, wait a minute," Hunter said. "What if something's wrong. We wouldn't know about it until it's too late." Screw that.

Bear nodded his head. "I think you're overreacting, but under the circumstances, I understand." He looked at Roc.

"Grow some wings, brother. Check in after you make contact."

"Oh *hell* no. If anybody's going, it's me," Hunter said. And no way was it going to be *Roc*.

"Can't let you do that. If you're the target, Rudolph could have his men lying in wait for you to show. Told you that before, and we're still not chancing it."

Hunter looked to the side and opened his mouth to tell Roc to keep his hands to himself, but the man was already gone. "Fuck." He raked his hand through his hair.

"Need you to keep it together," Bear said.

Hunter glared at him.

"How the hell am I supposed to do that, huh? My sister is in danger, and the woman I–I've been fucking has been lying to me, playing me."

"Told you to stay detached," Bear gently chided.

"Sorry, we can't all have hearts made of ice," Hunter spat. All sympathy faded from Bear's face.

"You don't know shit about me," Bear said, a whisper of warning.

"Enough," Brody said. "We all need to stay focused here."

Hunter wasn't feeling it. He turned on Brody. "Yeah, well tell me how to do that, because I ain't got any ideas." His heart was breaking, shattering as he pretended it wasn't really that bad.

It was so much worse than bad.

"You go back in there and act like everything is normal," Bear said.

"Fuck that," Hunter roared. No way could he pretend to her face that she wasn't some cold, conniving bitch who was out to ruin him, hurt his sister, tear apart his life. How he managed not to scream, he didn't know, but when he spoke next, it was with a calm he sure as hell didn't feel. "I'm going to talk to her. Confront her. Then I'll call Flint and have her thrown in jail."

He marched toward the door.

"Don't call the cops," Bear said. "Just keep her in the house."

"No promises." He was done with those.

———

MAYA SIGHED as she glanced at the clock. She had re-read the same chapter three times now, but still didn't understand it. She had a paper due on this book in a couple of weeks, so she didn't have time to read the same material over and over.

"You look frustrated," Hunter said. She looked up, but the smile she'd already been forming dropped from her face. He stood at the door, his hair matted as if he'd been wearing a cap, or running his fingers through it repeatedly. He sounded fine, but his eyes? They were all wrong. Dark, hollow. Bleak. There was something else there she couldn't quite put her finger on.

Sitting up, she asked, "What's going on?"

He shut the door and walked toward her, carrying some papers. He sat on the couch with her, but at the other end. It was as if he didn't want to sit near her.

She swallowed and leaned toward him. "Hunter?"

When he looked at her, she was close enough to pinpoint that other emotion. *Pain.*

He was hurting.

"What's wrong?" she asked.

"We've been investigating Jake." He shook his head, looking away from her and laughing humorously. *"Jake."*

"What did he do?" Oh god, was it bad? It had to be from the way Hunter looked. Did Jake break into her dorm room? Get to Heather?

"Nothing," Hunter breathed. Then he looked at her.

For some reason, she wished he hadn't. She fought the need to squirm in her seat. "I don't understand."

"Let's just cut the shit, and you tell me about that ten grand sitting in your savings account."

"What?" Maya balked. "What does that have to do with anything? And why are you looking into my account?" Her heart raced, blood pounding in her head.

"I didn't. The FBI did. They had their reasons, and they were obviously onto something."

He was almost too calm, staring at the papers in his hand. She looked closer and noticed on top were pieces of her note.

The one left on her car.

"You went through the trash?" she asked, standing slowly. How long had he known about it, and why did he have it now?

He lifted the paper and tilted it, letting the torn remnants fall to the ground while he held onto the bottom sheet. "No. But one of my guys did."

Then more silence.

He looked at her, pinning her with his gaze, and she shifted on her feet. "Look, I should've told you about the note being on my car, but it didn't mean anything important. It was just Jake being a jerk."

Uh-oh. Hunter stood slowly, his mask of indifference turning to rage.

"You think I give a *shit* about him?" he shouted. "He

wasn't the one who lied to me." He stabbed his finger against his chest, and Maya took a step back. Maybe withholding the information *could* be considered a lie, in a roundabout way, but even that was taking it to the extreme.

"If I'd thought it was important, I would have told you."

The skin between his brows wrinkled. "You think this is about the note."

It wasn't a question, but she answered anyway. "Yeah. I mean, why else would you be mad at me?"

"The. Money." He tilted his head like a puppy. An enraged puppy. "How easy was it? To whore yourself out for ten grand? Gotta say, honey, you sold yourself short."

She gasped. What the hell was wrong with him? And why would he call her such a thing? He was being a freaking jerk! "How dare you talk to me like that."

"How dare I?" He stomped toward her. "How dare *I*?"

"Yes. You asshole," she screamed in his face.

"That is fucking rich coming from you." He turned, walked away from her, running his hand through his hair.

One mystery solved. But not the important one. Her hands began to sweat and her eyes stung.

He'd called her a whore. It was slowly sinking in. The man she loved had called her a *whore.* She blinked rapidly and bit her lip to keep from crying. She didn't know what was going on with him, but she did not want to give him any ammunition. She took the quietest breath she could to calm her nerves and somehow managed to keep the tears at bay. When she knew she could talk without her voice breaking, she said, "I don't know what's gotten into you."

"You can't even admit it, can you?" he asked without looking at her.

"Admit what?"

"That you played me. Played my sister."

She opened her mouth, but she was too shocked to form words.

He turned around. "Yeah, I know. Alonzo Rudolph paid you off. But good job on pretending your ex-boyfriend was stalking you. Nice touch."

The pain she'd felt earlier immediately shifted to fury.

"You think I had my car vandalized?"

"Collateral damage." He shrugged. "You probably have a brand new one waiting for you back home. A present for a job well done." He winked at her, and it was a slice to the heart.

He really believed she had something to do with this mess. That Jake was a fake. She was too stunned to respond. Part of her wanted to defend herself. To explain that the money was a graduation gift from her uncle.

The other part, though, that part wanted to run, say *screw you,* and go back home, forget school.

Forget everything.

Hunter moved and her gaze darted to him. She watched as he pulled out a phone and called someone.

He stared right at her as he put the phone to his ear.

"I need you to pick her up for questioning. No, I can't. You'll have to do it. We're still at my house. *What?*" he yelled. "No, I haven't seen her. Maybe she's out with Roxie. Yeah. Okay. Thanks, man."

He ended the call and pocketed the phone.

"You're not my problem anymore."

"I never was your problem," she said, losing the battle with her tears.

"No, apparently, you weren't."

She blinked away the welling moisture.

"Don't," he barked. "Don't you fucking cry."

She sniffed in a deep breath and shrugged one shoulder

because she couldn't speak. She wished she wouldn't cry way more than he probably hoped she wouldn't.

"I'm done falling for your lies," he ground out. "You can tell the authorities and they can sort everything out."

"I never should've fallen in love with you."

His stone exterior cracked just a little. He opened his mouth, closed it, opened it again, but nothing came out.

A beeping sounded by the wall, and he shut his eyes slowly. When he walked toward the security panel, she covertly wiped her tears before he could witness that.

He pressed a button. "Yeah?"

"It's Flint. I was down by the Pattersons' farm when Gauge called. Said you needed me."

Hunter growled something before pushing some buttons and giving Flint the all clear. When he turned to face her, she erected her own walls around her heart and crossed her arms over her chest for added protection.

"That my ride?" she asked sarcastically.

"Yep," he said just as snidely.

"Good." She couldn't get away from this man soon enough.

When a knock sounded, Hunter opened the door.

"She's all yours."

The bastard couldn't even wait for the other man to enter all the way before he was ready to hand her off. To the police, no less. Wow. At least with Jake, she knew she was getting a control freak. Hunter just pretended to be nice. A wolf in sheep's clothing.

She was so caught up in her sense of betrayal that she didn't see the gun right away, and even then her brain was slow to process what was happening.

The man at the door had a gun. He was a cop, though, right? He was supposed to have one. But why was it in his hand and not in a holster? Had there been a threat out there? She didn't have a chance to ask.

He lifted the gun and blasted a shot, and through her screams, it barely registered that she'd never seen so much blood.

CHAPTER SIXTEEN

MAYA'S HEAD throbbed as she moved against something hard. Her body was like lead, and she was so exhausted. Groaning, she tried to move her hand to rub her aching forehead but it was stuck.

"Your wrists are tied," someone said. She was too tired to look, but the voice was familiar. Where was she at? "How's your head?"

"Feels like a pin cushion." If those pins were knives. And those knives were on fire.

"Brody is going to be so pissed," the voice breathed.

Maya cracked open an eyelid and saw Xan sitting across from her, covered in dirt. They were in some kind of a warehouse. *Why?* It hurt to think. She wanted to ask, but talking required energy.

"It's my fault." But the statement hadn't come from Xan. Maya glanced to the side, ignoring the stabbing pain in her temple, and found Roxie sitting there in the same condition as Xan. "I was the one who talked you into going to Hunter's to ask about Roc's barn."

"I knew better, though."

"Oh, please, it's not like you have to get permission to go anywhere. You and I run to town all the time." She huffed. "I didn't see the big deal in going to a *friend's* house to talk about wedding stuff."

"When that friend is watching over a witness or something, *working*, then yeah, he'd have a problem with it."

When had they been at Hunter's house? Maya didn't remember seeing them earlier.

"It's not like we haven't been there before."

"I know, girl," Xan said.

"I just don't understand why Flint would do this to us. My own flesh and blood," Roxie said, her voice quivering.

Flint. Right. Hunter had called him and wanted him to take her away. He'd believed she'd lied to him about Jake. She remembered that part, not that she wanted to remember it. But yeah, she remembered Hunter calling the man, and letting him in. Maya gasped.

"He shot Hunter." Oh god. She moved her arms around, trying to loosen the rope. "He had a gun and he shot him."

"Stop. That's some kind of voodoo knot," Roxie said. "You'll just tear your wrists up."

"I have to get to him. I have to help him." The fact that he was ready to throw her out of his house and out of his life didn't matter. He was hurt. She could be pissed later...after she knew he was okay. *Please, God, let him still be alive.*

"Help is on the way," Xan said.

Maya looked around the dark, dank warehouse and wondered how the woman was so sure of that. It was too dark to make out much, but it wasn't as if she heard the cavalry banging the door down. But Maya had been knocked out, so maybe she just wasn't up to speed on who was out there. "How do you know?"

Xan smiled at her then, as if she had some sixth sense, sabotaging any hope Maya felt. Had the woman cracked under pressure and lost her mind? Was that it? She was clearly delusional.

"Don't look at me like I'm crazy, girl. After some things went down with me before, Brody has all kinds of trackers on me." She lifted her shoe.

"It's hidden in the sole."

Yeah, the jury was still out on Xan's mental health.

"And they'll find Hunter before they find us because we were at his property when I hit my panic button on my phone."

"What?" Maya said, frowning at her.

"Jeez, woman, quit talking in circles," Roxie said, and then looked at Maya. "We showed up at Hunter's. Saw Flint's car there—personal, not squad—and as we walked up to the porch, we heard blood-curdling screams."

"He stuck me with something," Maya said, looking at her shoulder, but her sleeve covered the evidence.

"Xan fired off her S.O.S. flare thingy-ma-bob to Brody."

"We tried to make a run for it, but the door was open, and the screaming had stopped. He either saw us high-tailing it to the car or heard us running on the gravel. He shot out a tire on my car and told us not to move."

"He said he shot Hunter, and he'd shoot us, too," Roxie said, tears forming in her eyes.

Okay, so know she understood what they'd meant by being at Hunter's and why she hadn't seen them.

Maya's wrists burned. "Have you tried untying each other's wrists?"

Xan lifted her hands out from under the loose rope, and Maya gaped at her. "He ordered us to tie each other up, so we didn't tie them very tightly, but he did yours." She shrugged.

"After he was gone for a while, we undid ours and tried yours, but apparently, they teach proper abduction skills in the police academy," Roxie added, clearly upset about her cousin.

"All we were doing was irritating your skin, and we didn't want to make you start bleeding."

"At least *you* don't want to see me hurt," Maya mumbled as she looked away. She figured Hunter and his crew hadn't had a chance yet to spread their halfcocked theories to these ladies.

"What does that mean?" Xan asked.

Maya laughed bitterly. "Hunter thinks I have something to do with what's going on. He spouted off things like I'd played him, and some dude had paid me off to get to him."

"Why would he think that?" Roxie asked, narrowing her eyes. Great, she should've known they'd be more willing to take Hunter's side.

"Because he's an asshole."

Xan laughed. "They all can be. The whole lot of them. I think it's some requirement for their little club."

"Which is led by the king of assholes," Roxie muttered.

Maya relaxed a little when she realized the girls weren't going to quickly jump to Hunter's defense. "My uncle gave me ten-thousand dollars when I graduated high school. Hunter thinks it was someone else. That since I got the money when I went to college, it was some pay off for befriending Heather to get to him." She shook her head. "He called me a whore."

Xan gasped.

"Oh no, he didn't," Roxie said, full of sass.

"Yeah, he did."

"Why would he think you betrayed him?" Xan asked, no accusation in her voice, only curiosity.

"I honestly don't know. We really didn't get a chance to talk. He was too busy throwing around accusations and then throwing me out."

A loud bang sounded from outside and echoed all around them. The girls scrambled to put their hands through their ropes to make it look like they were still tied up and succeeded before the overhead door rolled up.

Four men came in, dragging people. Well, two pulled a limp and bloodied man, but the other two carried what looked like unconscious women. At least she hoped they were just unconscious. They were all unceremoniously dropped to the floor before the men took position on each side of the door. When the next person walked in, Maya gasped. She'd seen him before, sure, but it had been years.

"Uncle Al?"

He walked toward her with open arms, and she mutely watched as he placed his hands on her cheeks and kissed her forehead.

"You did an excellent job, *criado*. Excellent."

"I-I don't understand."

"I know, Maya. I know."

———

HE SAW the gun before Flint fully raised it, aiming it at him. He fell back before he could pull the trigger, but he wasn't fast enough. The bullet grazed his shoulder and blood gushed out of him. Not crying out was hard, but he had to save his own ass.

Alonzo had gotten to Maya and Flint. How the hell had he managed that? Hunter couldn't even begin to imagine.

Maya's screeching was a nice touch, but maybe she hadn't known Flint was going to shoot him. He couldn't see what was going on, but he figured they ran as soon as they could.

Another gun shot.

What the fuck?

"Don't move!"

Was Maya trying to get away? Maybe she didn't know Flint was working with her.

He crawled to the window with his good arm, staying down and out of enemy sight. Creeping up the wall, he carefully looked out. Maya was in the front seat, looking down, as Flint ordered Xan into the back of his car. Looked like Roxie was already in there. Shit.

He dug into his pocket for his phone, wishing he had his gun on him. He'd left his primary piece in the garage when he stormed in here to talk to Maya. He had another stashed in the kitchen. He'd missed a call from Brody a minute or so ago, so he hit that number as he ran toward the kitchen.

"What happened?" Brody barked while Hunter grabbed the gun.

"Can't talk now, bro. Flint's driving away with your woman."

"Flint?"

He heard a loud string of curses on the other end, but those hadn't come from Brody. It sounded like Bear.

Hunter ran to the door, gun drawn, safety be damned.

"Shit, I got taillights."

"Don't shoot," Brody roared.

"Not my first day," Hunter muttered as he ran to his truck, started it up, and pealed out.

"Hang back."

"What?" Hunter roared as he swerved to miss a dead possum. "You can't be serious. He has *Xan*."

"Fuck, *fuck,* I know. She has a tracker on her. Sent me a distress signal, so Bear and I headed your way immediately. We'll be at your place in less than two minutes. Bear's on the line with Roc, getting him back. Gauge was out digging more into Maya. He called reinforcements and is high-tailing it to meet up with us."

He knew Gauge was heavy into research when he'd called him to come get Maya. He'd told Hunter he'd send someone else out to get her. He didn't think he'd send Flint. That had been a surprise, but it shouldn't have been a big deal. Sure, Bear hadn't wanted the cops involved, but Flint was different. Or so they thought.

At the next corner, Brody's headlights flashed him. "Turn around," he barked, and threw up his hand as he passed Hunter.

He growled as he did a U-ey in the street and followed Brody back to his house.

When he jumped out of his truck, the other two guys were already waiting for him.

"I could've followed his ass," Hunter said.

"And then what? We can't just run him off the road. He has hostages. Besides, going in hotheaded isn't the answer." Bear cast Brody a lethal look.

"Not gonna apologize." Brody shrugged. "But you're trying my patience, man. He has my woman, and I'm not going to sit around with my thumb up my ass. I agreed to formulate a plan, but I didn't agree to wait."

Bear tilted his head to the side, cracking it. The man was obviously filled with tension. They all were.

"Look, there's something neither of you know about Flint."

"You two had some falling out. We know that," Brody said, his patience nonexistent.

"No." Bear shook his head. "I mean, yes, we did, but it's not that simple. Remember the drug bust we helped the feds with a couple of years back? The marijuana farm?"

"Yeah," Hunter said, crossing his arms.

"Local police got pulled in on that to contain the area."

"So," Brody said, getting even more agitated. They all remembered that.

"Some of the *evidence* didn't make it into custody."

"Meaning someone filched some pot for their personal stash," Hunter said slowly. It was illegal, sure, but a dime bag was hardly worth their time.

"Street value was estimated at over ninety grand, but that could've been a low number."

Hunter whistled low.

Brody's face grew dark. "Someone wanted to make some money."

"Bingo. Even though the feds knew Flint was involved, the evidence was circumstantial. They needed more to go on.

"And they tasked you with getting that evidence? Why? Hunter asked. "Because you two were close," he said, guessing.

"Not exactly."

"What does that mean?" Brody asked.

"If your best friend came into what he thought was a sweet little side-hustle, don't you think he'd want you to have a piece of the action?" Bear raised an eyebrow at him.

"Oh shit," Brody breathed.

"Yeah. When I said no, that was the end of our friendship. I should've turned him in then, but I...couldn't," Bear said, looking away. When he focused on the guys again, he said, "After everything went down with Colonel, I ratted him out, worried Colonel might've been connected somehow. Lord knows Flint isn't smart enough to be a ring-leader if there was more to this than what I knew about. But no link was found, and the weed was long gone by that time. They needed something more to go on." He sighed. "Since Gauge's agent status was known and I was in charge now, I pulled him in on this. He's been watching Flint's bank records, but hasn't found any evidence of the money."

"Why didn't you tell us before?" Brody asked.

Bear gritted his teeth. "Because it isn't an official job. It's fucking personal. We're not making any money off this. Even though I tried to right a wrong, the feds needed more to go on. It was my word against his. Gauge is doing this as he has time."

"We could've all helped," Hunter said. If they had, maybe they'd have found out the truth about him before he got a hold of Xan and Roxie. He didn't say that out loud, but Bear frowned at him as if he'd read his mind.

"Look, you better believe if I had *any* idea he was capable of more than selling drugs, I would've put the heat on him a long time ago. Figured out a way to run him out of town. *Something.*"

A horrible thought crossed Hunter's mind and he voiced it without thinking, "Does Roxie have anything to do with it?"

Brody's gaze flew to Bear's, a slight look of panic on his face. Hunter understood it had nothing to do with Roxie and Bear, although if Bear had suspected Roxie of anything, it could explain why he'd never let himself get close to her. No, Hunter knew the fear that landed on Brody's face was because his soon-to-be wife was best friends with Roxie. If Roxie was into something illegal, she'd have to distance herself from the woman, too, and it would crush Xan.

Bear blinked. Hesitated. Then gave his head a quick shake. "No."

"But you looked into that possibility," Brody said.

Bear glared at Brody, not answering, although it hadn't really been a question.

"Because Xan and Scott are around her all the time. They love her, man, and if there's any chance they could get in any kind of trouble because of her—"

"She checked out," Bear reiterated.

"You're gonna have to give me more than that. Her life is tangled up in all of ours."

"You have no idea just how much I know that," Bear said, leaning closer to the other man. Hunter and Brody stared at him, knowing full well what he meant.

Bear's phone rang. "It's Gauge," he said to the guys before answering and moving in closer. "Yeah?" He didn't say anything for several seconds. "I'm putting you on speaker."

"...landed at Conway airport forty minutes ago."

Bear looked up. "A private jet. Flight plan logged by Oberman," he mumbled.

Hunter put his hands on his hips. Was this Maya's getaway? Flint's?

"Since he's flagged, the FBI tracked it. But that's all they did. No one was on the ground to tail them."

Brody pulled out a hand-held device. "They're holding still at the old train depot just outside of Conway."

"Let's roll," Hunter said as he turned to jog toward his truck. "If they have a plane, they're ghosts."

"Fuck," Bear roared. "Gauge, meet us there. Call Roc. He should be nearing Mayflower now anyway. We'll rendezvous at the north tracks. And get the feds on this.

They wanted evidence against Flint–well, here they fucking go."

Within seconds, the guys were hitting the road again, but this time, Hunter wouldn't stop until he ended this. The pain he felt didn't matter. He had a job to do, and he would do it. Just like Bear had with Roxie.

He understood that man better now, why it seemed he had ice in his chest when it came to Roxie Willis.

It was to keep his heart numb.

CHAPTER SEVENTEEN

"Why are you here?" Maya asked, frowning at her uncle but stealing glances at her ex.

"Don't worry your pretty little head about that, dear."

The man who'd slumped against the wall spat out blood. "Your uncle's been a bad, bad man."

Maya squinted, trying to make out the person.

"Blade?" Xan asked. "Oh god, is that you?" Maya had only seen him a couple of times before, not that she'd be able to tell by the look of him anyway. He was covered in blood and bruises.

"Hi, doll," he said, tilting his head to the side and smiling at her. His teeth were all bloodied, too.

Roxie whimpered, and he winked at her, probably in an attempt to calm her down. Or so it looked to Maya. She couldn't really tell with this other eye swollen shut.

"You'd do well to shut your mouth, Mr. Young."

"That's my daddy's name, Al."

Her uncle strode over to Blade and raised the gun in his hand.

"No," Maya yelled, but it was too late; he hit Blade in

the face, knocking him down. He groaned, and she instinctively tried to get up, but failed. She found little comfort that her uncle had hit him with the gun. It could've been much worse. Was her uncle even capable of shooting someone? She feared she knew that answer already.

One of the other women groaned and rolled over. What she saw had her feeling the blood drain from her face; her body frozen in shock. Heather. He'd taken Heather. Her lip was cut up as if she'd been hit, and one of her arms, had moved at a weird, unnatural angle. Her body was bloody and broken.

"Oh my god," she breathed.

Uncle Al looked to the side. "She had a mouth on her, that one." He pointed to Heather and shook his head. "Should have killed her just for that. I needed her alive, though."

Tears streamed down Maya's face as she blinked up at her mother's brother. The man who'd always sent her birthday cards. The man her mother spoke fondly of. "Please," she whispered.

Jake groaned. "God, I've missed that word on your lips."

Bile rose in her mouth at the image his gross statement created.

Uncle Al snapped his fingers at Jake and shook his head like the man was being an annoying child who needed to be taken to task, and Jake quickly fell in line as if he strived for obedience and praise from the man. It was so surreal.

"Don't worry, child. You'll be fine. This has nothing to do with you." His uncle laughed. "Your mother will not be pleased with me, but she'll get over it. She always does."

"Your uncle is a monster," Blade muttered against the floor.

"Can I hit him again?" Jake asked, taking a step toward

Blade, but checking himself. It was obvious he didn't want to do anything without her uncle's approval.

"Shut up," the other woman on the floor hissed in Blade's direction. Maya's gaze flew to her, but she couldn't see her very clearly. She knew who it was, though. The only other person involved in this mess who hadn't been accounted for. Anna Sue. The FBI agent who'd been sent back to impersonate Maya.

Blade glanced at Anna Sue, and some emotion flashed in his eyes before he looked at Jake. "Give it your best shot, small fry."

Jake took two steps, ready to give Blade just what he sarcastically asked for.

"Jake," Uncle Al barked. The guy almost pouted as he stepped back to the spot he'd been standing before, minding like a good little dog. God, why did she ever think him attractive?

"What your uncle doesn't want you to know is that he paid lover boy over there to date Heather, but when that didn't work, he ordered him to fuck you over, literally," Blade said, struggling to sit back up and panting as he did so. "Heather posted some photo online of her in her cap and gown with her proud brother, Hunter, by her side. Alonzo's people discovered it, and he set the plan into motion. Figured out where Heather was going to attend college, and planted you there."

Maya shook her head. "No." That couldn't be true. Her family had always been strict, straight-laced, and very stern. She'd had to talk to them for weeks about attending an out-of-state college. After all that time, they still almost hadn't gone for it. "That's crazy."

"I'm afraid it's true," her uncle said. "Don't you remember when I visited you that summer how I talked about how great Texas was? I was the one who put the idea of that school in your head. When your mother didn't want you to go, I assured her you'd be watched over."

"But, but they called you Alonzo Rudolph-something-or-other," Maya stammered, still not wanting to believe what she was hearing. It didn't make any sense.

"I took that surname long before you were born. Couldn't have my enemies coming after my sister, now could I?"

The gravity of the situation slowly sank in as she mulled over his words and took stalk of who all was in the room. He uncle had set her up. He'd been behind all of this. He really *was* a bad man. Evil. Vile. So much worse than she'd ever thought Jake even was.

And everyone battered, bloodied, and broken slumped around on the floor was here because of her uncle.

Because of Maya.

Because she'd been so naïve she couldn't see what kind of man her uncle was or that he'd use her like this.

She should've seen the signs, but she hadn't. Now, people who'd tried to help her, who'd trusted her, had been deceived. Many were held captive right here. Another one possibly dead. This was an utter nightmare.

And it was all her fault.

HUNTER LOOKED out the side window as they slowed to a stop near the old train depot. He watched for any signs of activity around the building, but he saw nothing. That didn't mean no one was out there, though.

"Roc, you almost here?" Bear asked over the phone.

"Twenty-two seconds."

"Get Gauge on the line," Bear said to the guys in the vehicle. "We need to know how close he is."

Hunter made the quick call. He figured Brody wouldn't be patient enough to deal with communication. The man looked ready to bolt to the building and get his woman.

"Gauge, what's your twenty?" Hunter asked as soon as the other man picked up.

"Right behind you. You're gonna wanna hear this." He ended the call before Hunter could ask for more details.

Looking out the side window, he watched as Gauge pulled up beside them. The man killed the engine, got out, and slipped into the vehicle with the others.

"Blade activated his emergency comms." He started fiddling with the knobs on the hand-held radio. "He's inside."

"What the hell is he doing here?" Hunter barked. He was supposed to watching his sister.

"Sounds like he didn't come willingly," Gauge said grimly.

Ice cold fear drenched Hunter. "Heather," he breathed. If Maya hurt one hair on her head, he'd kill her himself. The stabbing pain he got in that moment was because of the fear he had for his sister. He wouldn't allow it to be about anything else.

Blade's voice suddenly came through the radio, "... Uncle doesn't want you—"

"Turn, it up," Bear whispered heatedly.

"...He paid lover boy over there to date Heather, but when that didn't work, he ordered him to fuck you over, literally."

Blade stopped talking and it sounded like he was struggling to breathe.

"Shit, we gotta move."

A car came running up toward them. Hunter grabbed his gun on instinct, but before he could move into a defensive position, Roc jumped out and yanked their door open.

"He's got Heather."

Blade's voice came back. "Heather posted some photo online of her in her cap and gown with her proud brother, Hunter, by her side. Alonzo's people discovered it, and he set the plan into motion. Figured out where Heather was going to attend college, and planted you there."

"Fuck!" Hunter banged the dashboard. He should've known something would happen to her out of state. He should've never let her go back to school.

"I'm getting her back from that conniving little bitch," Hunter muttered before jumping out of the car.

"No, man," Gauge said as he, Bear, and Brody got out and rounded the vehicle. "It sounds like she doesn't know what's going on."

"What?" Hunter asked, frowning, his head reeling. "If she didn't know then that means—"

"No," Maya's breath came though the radio now. "That's crazy."

"I'm afraid it's true," Alonzo said. "Don't you remember when I visited you that summer how I talked about how great Texas was? I was the one who put the idea of that school in your head. When your mother didn't want you to go, I assured her you'd be watched over."

"But, but they called you Alonzo Rudolph-something-or-other," Maya stammered.

"Jesus Christ," Hunter breathed before grabbing the hair on top of his head and stumbling back. "She didn't know. Fuck me, she didn't know." He'd accused her of being behind all of this.

He'd called her horrible names.

He'd been ready to fucking kill her for putting Heather in danger.

God, what had he done?

"Deal with it later," Brody snapped. "Xan is in there, and I ain't heard her speak yet. I'm goddamn done waiting."

He took off with Roc on his heels. With the shock of this revelation, Hunter was the last to find his feet, but with fear and rage fueling him, he ran, passing everyone else on his team.

The fear was for the women.

The rage, though? That was directed at himself.

CHAPTER EIGHTEEN

EVERYTHING HAPPENED SO FAST.

The window in the corner behind Maya shattered so quickly that if she hadn't been facing it, she'd have missed it. Luckily, she hadn't been close enough to be hit by flying glass.

Before anybody could react to whatever was happening, smoke filled the room.

"Fire," Jake shouted, but Maya didn't think fire could cause that much smoke immediately like that.

Then again, what did she know about anything?

"Anna," Blade roared, and the intensity of his tone had Maya scrambling for cover, not that she could move much.

Gunfire erupted around her. She was nothing more than a sitting duck in the middle of all this chaos.

Whatever movies made people believe about slow motion in a life-or-death situation was completely true. Didn't matter that everything was happening incredibly fast around her. Time stood still for Maya. All her motions were slow, exaggerated, as glass-filled debris flew through the air.

She ducked, trying to cover her head as best she could as the door blasted off its railing and more shots rang out.

People shouted, but she couldn't make out any words. Within moments, a body dropped beside her. One of the guys who'd been guarding the door now had a bullet in his head.

She shook all over and bit her lip to keep from screaming out. Whatever was happening, she didn't want to draw attention to herself.

"Maya!" Now she was hearing things. Hunter's voice in her mind helped drown out the noise around her. It was a welcomed distraction among the death and mayhem. "Maya!"

She looked up, not believing she'd see him, but needing to know what was happening. The gunshots had slowed and she was still breathing. That had to be a good sign, right?

Like a dark savior, Hunter materialized from the smoke, running toward her.

"Hunter?" she breathed, not loud enough for her own ears. He was really here. But why was he calling her name?

Had he come to have her arrested?

"You okay, baby?"

Baby? Her mind was too frazzled to comprehend him. Maybe she was in shock because no way had she heard him right.

"Heard everything off Blade's transmitter once we got in range. Fucker started talking as soon as we made contact, so we'd know what was going on. Stay down." He turned his head away from her with his hand to his ear as he said, "Affirmative. Where's my sister?"

The smoke thinned a little as another shape took form. Maya opened her mouth, but fire popped from the figure before she could make a sound. Hunter jerked and fell over.

Maya screamed as blood splattered across her face.

"I'm hit," Hunter muttered, but she knew. It was why she'd started screaming. And hadn't stopped.

Uncle Al leaned over and smacked her. "Shut up." She blinked in shock as she rubbed her cheek. "Well, *criado*, we meet again. I knew we would one day."

"You didn't have to come all the way out here to see me," he said as he gripped his chest, panting. "Postcard would've worked."

Alonzo laughed. "You always did have a humorous streak."

"Know what else I always had?" Hunter asked as he winced.

"What?" The smile left Maya cold. But the gun he lifted had her flinching, wanting to do something. Anything. Hunter covertly grabbed the side of her leg to keep her still.

"A faster hand." He moved so quickly that she never saw the gun, only heard the shot. Her uncle fell to his knees, his eyes glazing over in death, as blood leaked from a hole between them.

Three more shots fired in the distance.

"Where's Flint?" Bear yelled.

"No sign of him," someone else answered.

"Clear," an agent shouted, followed by a chorus of others. Hunter sat up, ripped his shirt open, and grabbed at the straps underneath. The breath *whooshed* out of her lungs. He'd worn a bulletproof vest. He'd be okay.

The haze around them drifted up, revealing the bodies scattered around on the floor. Maya moved her wrists, trying to break free of the binding, fear crashing over her. It was silly that she felt herself freaking out now that the shooting had stopped. It didn't matter, though; she had to get up now. Get away. Breathe clean air.

I've never seen dead people before. She couldn't look at her uncle or she'd throw up. Yes, she need clean air right now.

"Stop, stop," Hunter said as he grabbed her arms, stilling her. "You're bleeding." He dug in his boot, pulled out a knife, and cut the rope. "Take a deep breath. You're okay now." Then he turned to the side and yelled, "Heather? Where's my goddamn sister?" as he looked around.

"Got her!"

Maya looked in the direction of the voice and saw Roc bending over Heather, stroking her hair.

"C'mon," Hunter murmured, pulling Maya up beside him. He wrapped an arm around her and tugged her along with him. Maya's gaze darted around the room, and amid the men with bold letters on their jackets were the guys she'd met at the garage, most of them tending to those who'd been captured.

Blade fussed over Anna, but she kept swatting him away. Maya figured there was much more to the agent than most people saw.

Brody kissed Xan.

Bear sat on the floor, his arms around Roxie, rocking her gently back and forth. She wasn't crying. She seemed to be staring off into space in shock. Still, Bear looked ready to murder anybody in the room who dared to looked at her.

As they neared where Heather was on the floor, Hunter stiffened and Gauge gaped. Roc's head was bent near Heather, his hand on her cheek as she cried, sobs tearing through her as if a part of her soul had died. And this man, that she got the feeling most of the guys didn't like, was sitting beside her.

Consoling her.

It was something, she figured, he wasn't used to doing, given the look on Gauge's shocked face.

"You can back away now," Hunter said, low and lethal.

Roc looked up, and Maya knew her own shock was evident at this point. His eyes were red, as if he was fighting tears. *Tears.* She knew very little about these men, but even the few times she was around Roc, he'd thrown off the don't-fuck-with-me vibe. Seeing him battling emotions was extremely odd. Almost as odd as how he hovered over Heather, as if he was shielding her from the world.

"I will fucking gut you, brother, if you try to make me," Roc said.

"Hey, hey," Gauge said, stepping between them. "We're all just worried."

Brody came up beside them, holding Xan's hand. He clapped Gauge on the shoulder. "Damn fine shooting. You took out three of those guards, man."

"No choice, brother. No choice."

"Paramedics are here," one of the agents announced.

Heather moved, and Roc wrapped his arms around her to help. Hunter let go of Maya and grabbed his sister from the other side, easing her up and away from Roc.

Heather huffed. "Jeez, Herman, stop."

"Herman?" several people said. Maya was one of them.

"Godammit, Heather." Hunter's cheeks turned slightly pink.

Brody laughed. "Why didn't we know your real name? That's priceless."

"No way in hell can you start calling me that," he grumbled.

"He's always gone by Hunter," Heather answered. "But calling him Herman gets his attention."

"That's almost as bad as Gauge's," Brody said.

"Don't," Gauge barked. "My handle has been a godsend."

Maya watched as Hunter pulled Heather closer to him. It was obvious he wanted to protect his sister, but it seemed he was overly concerned with protecting her from his teammate.

"I'm not a chew toy." Heather yanked her arm away and stumbled. Roc jumped and caught her before she could fall.

"I said back *the fuck* off," Hunter yelled, glaring at Roc. He clearly took any touching on Roc's part as manhandling.

"Let him help her," Brody urged.

Hunter looked at him, ready to argue, but then his gaze shifted to Maya. He blinked a few times; whatever fight he felt toward Roc she could tell was fleeing from his stern face. When he closed the few steps that were between them, she braced herself for whatever he was going to say now that the adrenaline from moments ago was dwindling.

Maya quickly threw a shield over her heart. For some reason, it had gotten knocked off during the gunfight, and hers hadn't been the only one. She was sure the *baby* comment had been a slip, that or he was being nice until he got his sister out of harm's way. She had no idea. There could've been any number of excuses why. Whatever the reason it had been was temporary. That battle hadn't changed the war in her heart, nor had it changed what'd happened earlier.

Hunter had accused her of some awful things.

Had called her names.

Wouldn't listen to her.

Had thrown her out of his house.

He'd been completely and totally unreasonable.

A brutish bad boy not listening to a woman who he

acted like he cared about. Those feeling of affection had been fine with him until they no longer suited him.

If he cared about her, he would've tried hearing her side of things rather than jumping to judgment.

"C'mon, let's get you checked out," Hunter said as he put an arm around her. He nudged her to walk, so she did. Not because she wanted to do what he asked, but because the faster she complied, the sooner she could get away. Maybe he wanted to talk to her alone. Maybe he wouldn't want to talk to her at all. Whatever it was, she'd get through this and move on. She couldn't deny his touch was comforting in the midst of this mess, but she couldn't rely on it. She wouldn't.

As far as she was concerned, nothing had changed between her and Hunter. And because of what happened to Heather, it wasn't as if she could just go back to school or move back in with her. Too much had happened. She honestly didn't know if she could ever show her face around school again.

First chance she got, she was flying home. She never should have left the protective bubble.

No matter how big of a lie it was. Her mother would be crushed to learn the truth, but at least Maya could be there for her.

She had nowhere else to be.

Hunter looked toward Roc and said, "Don't you get any ideas," as they walked away.

"Ideas are all I got, brother. All I got."

Hunter growled something, but didn't stop. Maya knew that wouldn't be the end of it. Not that she'd be around to see how it all worked out. She was just glad Heather had people who cared about her that'd help her heal. She was going to miss her friend.

CHAPTER NINETEEN

HUNTER STARED at the unassuming house. He wasn't sure how long he'd sat outside in his rental car, looking at it, trying to decide which bedroom belonged to Maya. He'd decided it was the second window on the top floor since the light had been on all morning. Jesus, that made him sound like a stalker.

It'd been three weeks since he'd shot her uncle, but this wasn't his first trip to her hometown.

No, not because he was a stalker. He'd shown up for the memorial service.

Oh, the deceased had been identified as Alonzo Rodriguez, not Alonzo Rudolph, but Hunter knew what man was being mourned. The real man. He hadn't shown up to grieve. He'd come to pay his respects to Maya. After all, he'd been the one to kill the man.

Maya had been shocked to see him, but she'd been cordial. Any chance to speak to her alone, however, was shot down with the words, "We have nothing to say to each other."

He had plenty to say, but he knew she hadn't been

ready to hear. Hell, she might not be ready now, but Hunter was tired of waiting.

Not that he'd sat idly by and done nothing. He wasn't a complete idiot—contrary to his actions. He'd gotten Heather to call her numerous times, and over the last week, the two had made some headway. He'd even overheard Heather laughing while on the phone with Maya. One of the many perks of having his sister being back home. She'd tested out early due to "medical" reasons. He knew Maya had also. The school couldn't say much since the FBI had backed up the girls' stories. Heather had decided to transfer back to Arkansas. It had been easier than he'd planned it would be, talking her into it. Having her close to him again was one less worry.

He had no idea what Maya had planned on doing. He'd asked Heather, but she'd spouted off some girl code bullshit, not wanting to ruin their healing friendship. He really couldn't blame her for that.

If he wanted to find out, he needed to get out of this car and go talk to her himself.

Taking a deep breath, he pushed himself out of the car and walked up the sidewalk to her house.

He knocked on the door and mentally calculated the seconds it'd take for her to come downstairs and answer it.

A minute ticked by.

Two.

He knocked again.

Nothing.

He stepped back and looked up at the window, knowing she had to be in there. The curtain had shifted to the side, and taking a chance, he waved.

The material fell back. Fighting a laugh, he bounded up the steps again and knocked. "I know you're in there."

This time, he heard her running down the stairs. Then a weird thump.

"Ow."

"Maya?"

She yanked open the door, holding her knee. "What?"

He did laugh then. "You are the most accident-prone woman I know. You okay?"

She dropped her foot to the floor and stood straight. "Never better," she said sweetly as she crossed her arms.

"Do you care if I come in?"

"Yes," she said, narrowing her eyes.

"Can I come in anyway?"

She sighed, dropping her head.

"I just want to talk," he said softly.

"I don't want to talk to you."

He didn't want her to feel forced, but god, he wanted to talk to her. He'd try a different tactic. "You don't have to. Can you just hear me out?"

After what felt like an eternity, she stepped back and motioned for him to come inside. She shut the door behind him and leaned against it, not inviting him in any farther.

He guessed he'd have to do this here. Standing in a foyer was better than trying to talk to her over the phone.

"I worked for Alonzo Rudolph."

Her eyes widened a little. She was a smart woman, so Hunter had no doubt she knew there was some connection between her uncle and him. His past, though, had been erased, and it wasn't as if her uncle had time to go into any details the day Hunter had killed him.

Without saying another word, she walked into a room off the hall, and he followed her. She sat on a small couch. He debated taking the chair across from her, but decided against it. If he never saw her again, he didn't want his last vision of her to be from across the room.

When he sat beside her, she shifted, crossed her legs, and stared at him wearily. "When was this?"

"A long time ago." He bent over, resting his elbows on his knees, watching his hands. "I was young and stupid. Out for a quick buck. But I learned the life wasn't for me and got out before I got too far in."

"That's pretty vague," she mumbled.

He blew out a breath. "I'm ashamed of it, okay? Did he have me kill anybody? No. But I was ordered to rough them up, maim them when they crossed him. Hell, even if they were a day late on a payment. No one fucked with Alonzo."

"So I figured out." She rolled her eyes. "You could've just had your sister tell me this when she called."

He didn't respond to that. Instead, he said, "I've had nightmares for years. Memories of the things he made me do. No," he said quickly. "Things I *did*. I carry that blame, and I knew one day it'd all come back to haunt me in real life, not just while I slept. Maya," he breathed.

Slowly, she looked at him.

"I never once planned on finding you. I never wanted to have someone in my life, because of my past. It didn't feel safe. I didn't feel worthy. Many reasons." He tilted his head, watching her. "But I did find you, and I don't want to let you go."

Fire lit behind her eyes. It was the first indication that all was not lost. The woman was pissed, and that was an emotion he could work with. It sure as hell was better than indifference.

"Well you should have thought about that before you hurled accusations my way and called me names." She jumped up.

He stood but didn't move toward her. "You're right. There is no excuse strong enough to explain why I acted like that. To me, it felt like the man I'd run from for years was back, and he didn't just want to end me, he wanted to make me suffer." He shook his head. "When I thought you betrayed me like that... You have no idea how much it killed me. I knew then Alonzo could win because if that was the truth, then he already had. I love my sister, but you, Maya, you were becoming my *life*. If something happened to Heather, I'd be devastated, yes, but I'd learn to deal. You're different," he said softly.

"You hurt me," she said softly.

"I know." He cleared his voice. "And I'll grow old and die regretting that. Doesn't change how sorry I am. Doesn't change that I love you so much it fucking scares me."

She stared at him, wide-eyed.

"Yeah, baby, I love you."

"Hunter." She shook her head. "I don't know if I—"

He couldn't hear those words. Not yet. If she was going to turn him away, he had to buy some time, find a way to mend the damage he'd caused.

Or find the strength to let her go.

He moved toward her and took her face between his hands.

"I'm sorry," he whispered before kissing her lightly. "I'm sorry," he said again before taking her bottom lip between his. "I'm so fucking sorry," he breathed before taking her mouth fully. He kissed her deeply, needing her to feel even a fraction of how much she meant to him.

When she kissed him back, his heart soared.

They kissed as they caressed, neither seeming ready to end it, but Hunter knew if he didn't stop soon, he'd take her right there on her parents' living room floor. He dropped a few light, teasing kisses before he rested his head on top of hers. "Please say you forgive me."

"I need time, I think."

The stabbing pain was much worse than he'd anticipated.

"Take all the time you need," he whispered.

She looked up at him, and he wasn't sure where he found the strength not to crush his lips to hers again.

"It's just that I've had this crazy fantasy about bad boys because of the sheltered life I've had, but it turns out my family is filled with them. I've been lied to enough already."

His heart broke with every word, but he wouldn't pressure her. He kissed her forehead and tried easing away from her, but she tightened her hold.

"Where are you going?"

"Er." *To drink myself silly and cry myself to sleep.* No way would he admit that.

"You got to talk. Now it's my turn."

"Okay."

Her shoulders lifted with the big inhale she took. "My life is crazy right now, but I love you—"

"Maya." He leaned toward her.

"No, wait." She put her hand on his chest. "I love you, Hunter. I do. But I need to go slow. There are things I need to re-learn, but I don't want to do that all alone," she said softly, looking away.

He slipped his hand onto her chin and urged her to look at him. "You aren't alone. Even if you send me away right now, you will never be alone." He smiled. "And I mean that in a non-stalkerish way."

She laughed softly.

"God, I've missed you." He pulled her into his arms and held her tightly. "I've thought about you every second."

"I'm sorry I haven't talked to you sooner. My mom has been depressed. My dad has been acting weird. School has been–"

"You don't need to apologize. I know you have a lot to deal with."

As he held her, he knew things would be okay with them. It might take some time. Years, maybe, as she finished school, and found her way on her own terms, but one day, they'd be right.

"Hunter?" she said softly.

"Yeah, baby."

"Conway has a college."

He smiled so hard his face hurt, but he tried not to squeeze her too hard or make any sudden movements. "More than one."

"You think Heather would like a roommate?"

Leaning back to look into her eyes, he said, "I think I'm going to have to beat up a lot of college boys in Faulkner County."

"There's only one bad boy I want."

"You have him, baby. You have him."

EPILOGUE

Three weeks ago

ANNA DOVE beside a shipping container as the gunfire erupted, intent on covering Heather since she was closest.

Her ankle had other ideas.

Pain shot through her leg as her foot stayed wedged under a pipe coming up through the floor. Definitely not going to win any medals for this rescue attempt. She screamed out in pain, uttering a few choice curses in the process.

"Anna," Blade shouted, and like a blond Greek god, he materialized. Even the pain from breaking her ankle while taking fire couldn't calm her body's response to him.

"I broke it," she wheezed.

"Oh shit, babe."

"Don't call me that," she said heatedly as she grabbed her ankle. Being so close to him during this assignment had been torture. The guy liked to walk around in nothing but his boxer briefs. She didn't know a man's body could be that cut in real life. V's were things of fantasy, right? Wrong. So, so wrong.

Or so, so right, depending on what mood she was in.

And the sweet name-calling hadn't helped her state of mind at all.

"Stay down," he barked. "I don't want you to get hurt."

What? She hadn't been the one antagonizing the sadistic murderer. Though the retort died on her tongue as her ankle seized on her. "Oh god."

Blade's carefree attitude faded into genuine concern. Yep, and that was even hotter.

She hated him a little bit more.

"Let me help you up. The ambulance should be here any second." He reached for her, and she slapped his hand away.

"I can get up myself."

"You're hurt."

"I'm fine." It was just a little broken. No biggie. She couldn't show weakness, especially around so many other agents. She was a professional woman. In a man's world.

And she sure as hell couldn't lean on Blade. The guy had more notches on his belt than rocks in the river, and in this small town, people talked. She couldn't risk any negative backlash. Besides, Blade wasn't one to settle down. Every woman in a forty-mile radius knew that. Yeah, getting drunk and having hot monkey-sex with Blade was out of the question. Period.

End of story.

She had to get that through her thick skull. She could not have sex with him.

At least, not again.

———

HEY, y'all!

Thank you for reading my book. :) If you enjoyed it, I'd be very grateful for a review. If you didn't like it, then share that, too... as long as your review is honest, that's all that matters.

And ice cream. Ice cream matters, too.

Want the latest scoop? Be sure to sign up for my News-letter! I mean, it's not as yummy as ice cream, but nothing ever is.

XOXO,
    Mandy

WANT MORE? Be sure to preorder **Blade**!

ABOUT THE AUTHOR

 Mandy Harbin is a *USA Today* Best-selling author who loves creating stories that explore the complexities of everyday relationships...with some kissing thrown in. She is a Superstar Award recipient, Reader's Crown and Passionate Plume finalist, and has achieved Night Owl Reviews Top Pick distinction many times. She also writes young adult romance as M.W. Muse because teens like kissing, too.

After graduating college and working many years in technology, she threw caution to the wind and began studying writing at the UALR. Years of trashed manuscripts and rejections eventually led to contracts and representation. With over thirty books published, she now serves on the board of her local writing chapter.

Mandy lives in a small, Arkansas town with her husband and their bossy dog, enjoying her own happily ever after...with some kissing thrown in.

mandyharbin.com/newsletter
facebook.com/Author.MandyHarbin
instagram.com/mandy_harbin
bookbub.com/authors/mandy-harbin

CPSIA information can be obtained
at www.ICGtesting.com
Printed in the USA
LVHW091027061020
668080LV00001B/360

9 781941 467206